RU

■ □ ■ □ ■

MARIAN PANKOWSKI

RUDOLF

Translated by John and Elizabeth Maslen

NORTHWESTERN UNIVERSITY PRESS

EVANSTON, ILLINOIS

Northwestern University Press
Evanston, Illinois 60208-4210

Originally published in Polish in 1980 by Oficyna Poetów i Malarzi,
London. Copyright © 1980 by Marian Pankowski and Poets' and
Painters' Press. English translation copyright © 1996 by Northwestern
University Press. Published 1996. All rights reserved.

Printed in the United States of America

ISBN CLOTH 0-8101-1417-8
ISBN PAPER 0-8101-1418-6

Library of Congress Cataloging-in-Publication Data

Pankowski, Marian.
  Rudolf / Marian Pankowski ; translated by John and
Elizabeth Maslen.
      p.   cm. — (Writings from an unbound Europe)
  ISBN 0-8101-1417-8 (alk. paper). — ISBN 0-8101-1418-6
(pbk. : alk. paper)
  I. Maslen, John. II. Maslen, Elizabeth. III. Title. IV. Series.
PG7158.P2R84 1996
891.8'537—dc20   96-9840
                                                              CIP

The paper used in this publication meets the minimum requirements of
the American National Standard for Information Sciences—Permanence
of Paper for Printed Library Materials, ANSI Z39.48-1984.

■ □ ■ □ ■

ON READING RUDOLF

An Open Letter to Marian Pankowski

Dear Professor,

Rudolf has been with us now for just over a year, and every reading of your work has been an enriching experience. We wanted to sum up for you what has impressed us most and what has made your work such a privilege and challenge to translate. The question is, where to begin?

Because *Rudolf* breaks so much fresh ground. Does one begin with a view of the novel as a repository of ideas or as a prose poem, brilliantly combining colloquial style with a wide range of imagery, where seriousness, wit, fantasy, farce, and finely controlled pathos are harnessed with passion and vigor—above all with a mastery of word and phrase, of constant sensitivity to the considerable resources of the Polish language, both literary and colloquial, but with a constant awareness of how to use them in fresh and daring ways.

Word and phrase must, we think, come first. Because *Rudolf* is indeed both novel and prose poem; and this means that words are used with a fine sense of their natural rules and rhythms in Polish, while also being quarried to bring their etymological potential to light. Dead metaphors are revived and envigorated while new images are offered; words and phrases are woven through the book as "clues," as threads to be followed. And we ignore these clues at our peril if the full richness of the work and of the ideas in the work are to be fully appreciated. The language ranges through the gamut of literary rhetoric (astutely used at moments of intensity) to children's rhyme and folk idiom—and innovation. The dominant tone of the work is colloquial, following speech rhythms but not becoming imprisoned by them: rhyme, assonance, and wordplay never let us forget that great literature must rest on the handling of language if it is to be great. And *Rudolf* is a feast of language.

We stress this because, on first reading, it is easy to be carried away by the power and vigor of the ideas, by their mode of presentation. Because while *Rudolf* is a prose poem, it also strikes blow after blow at our complacencies. For instance, "What is love?" Bacon's Pilate might have asked when he "would not stay for an answer." But *Rudolf* will not let us get away with this. Time and again we are challenged in our views of socially acceptable "norms": love and lust meet, conflict, merge, and are redefined; love of one's traditional and personal roots is set against the tyranny of the past; both powerful and wily characterization is used brilliantly, to make us unsure of our yardsticks. Eroticism is the most immediate and impressive weapon *Rudolf* uses on us, but this weapon, in turn, is used for and against the characters as well as the readers. And it is never a gimmick, never superficial. A very large part of the human comedy is played on this battlefield, with sensitive touches of finely wrought tragedy. Beauty and ugliness in all parts of our existence are tested against each other, yet we are never subjected to didacticism. Whenever we have a passage of intense argument, it will be skillfully undercut by what precedes or follows. In short, the reader is treated as an adult, invited to think and feel; and it is part of the work's construction to remind the reader that art is a fabrication, subject to our own as well as to the author's control and caprice.

W. H. Auden frequently used the idea of Prospero and Ariel to suggest the delicate balance between ideas in a literary work and the artistry of their expression. *Rudolf,* it seems to us, achieves this balance while never letting us forget that where Ariel is, where Prospero is, Caliban must be, too.

Translating *Rudolf* has been a superb and humbling experience. As you yourself say, Professor, toward the end of your book, all words have their own home. We have tried to construct a home that is for the English speaker what yours is for the Polish speaker. And our one hope is that we have been adequate stewards of so valuable a trust.

John and Elizabeth Maslen
September 27, 1984

RUDOLF

Poetry . . . Wounded lark that sheds blood through the skies . . .

To Vladimir Dimitrievic in true friendship

■ □ ■ □ ■

LITTLE BIRCH TREES ARE GRAY-SKINNED. AN ABSURD USE OF color for depicting young creatures. The urge for order and security increases with age. In spring everything ought to be utterly green: water that falls from the skies, ground thrusting out firm irises, and even the postman, who offers you letters in the selfsame hand that's barely emerged from the bud . . . But summer . . . in summer let's be the color of bilberries, of jet-black horses treading black plums from an inkwell upturned on a notebook. In this way grayness might be eliminated . . .

These reflections, because for some time now my mind's eye hasn't stopped filming the head of that fellow over there, who, at a table outside a café, holds high in the May air a wasps' nest cobbled together from rags and blues not entirely bleared by rheum.

A tourist in his seventies. How many first snows has he seen by now, how many first storks, first loves, and look at him now fallen into a crevice, stretched out at the bottom, watching the way his hairs wriggle out of his skin. A wolf, balding.

Let's bet he used to play in an orchestra. He must have been a drummer, because the head on his tankard of beer barely shows above his huge fingers . . . Suppose by this time . . . his drum's clinging to a song that's gone slack.

The tables are white, but the wall behind them is black

and gold, because we're on the Grand'Place in Brussels. And the man in question is sitting ten yards away from us wrapped in parchment, the work of some shady tanner.

And as for us, we're pretending to search earnestly for something on the upper stories, on the balconies where a lady of rank used to lay her freckled hands. But we're well aware that this man's very close. As for him, he's looking at his beer. Then at someone bearded, in green with a check-ered sky-blue tent on his back, striding across the Grand'Place. He looks at this American till he rounds the street corner . . . And so the tourist's gray head turns, turns on its slow hinges and stops. Stops because, opposite, two boys have materialized in shirts of Indian cotton, unbut-toned to the waist, molded into their jeans. And he looks at them as, with a sidelong glance, they dust off historic stone. Are they going to stay? Yes . . . And they've noticed this gray-haired man, eyes gazing at their Maytime open-breast-edness. But they don't see that I'm having a good look, too. That I'm positively staring at them. And so there we are, linked in a triangle by that human curiosity without which life would be as wretched as a blood sausage taken cold, without vodka.

And this septuagenarian with the face of a cauliflower from some outlying kitchen garden alongside a coalfield sits ridiculously rigid. And no one knows he's called Thomas. And that his time's in the process of expanding, dilating . . . Spiders' webs throw off their dust, their past calendars, and rainbow tinted, sky blue, return to the anal sally port of the spider who keeps watch at the gates of youth. He doesn't see the clinging jeans anymore because he's wiping his brow with his thick fingers, wiping his monumental nose and on either side of it those things so nearly like a herbarium's for-get-me-nots. His eyes have glazed over. His lens has focused on infinity.

And behind the old blighter's eyes . . . A haze, cut in uneven strips by the apprentice shears of some young Jewish tailor, drifts above a road where morning dust waits for the first peasant cart. What's that? Something that rumbles, growls, and snorts . . . and proclaims itself by trumpet blast. A sports car, with two men inside, wearing plus fours and leather jackets. And soft caps, because twenty miles an hour means nothing to them! So that a jay takes fright and starts to screech raucously. And they drive, drive, and snuff the tiny carpet of wild thyme that someone or other's beating in front of their noses to rid it of night's feathers.

"*Schööön* . . . ," they sigh in unison, and look at each other, thrilled by their unanimity. Groves of birch, fir, and rowan, upright and decked out in greenery, only smelling bitterly of betrothals on the eve of a war . . . smelling as bitterly as . . .

. . . this beer alongside the ramshackle hand of the old man, who's just sighed deeply, brought his eyes into play, and immediately started looking for those two in jeans . . . But before the gray lens has refocused on this day of May in the gilded Grand'Place of Brussels, this day where we're enmeshed—he, you, and I, I down there and I talking to you here—all that remains in the square is a group of African tourists in such tight shoes and such tight neckties that their heads have all but split open so as to let them ascend beyond the tower of the Hotel de Ville, right up to heaven on porcelain eyes.

Well—maybe I could sit down. Because I do actually belong here. Maybe I could, beside this elderly man . . . Because, after all, for my part, I know nothing of this sports car that startles jays, this spiderweb that drained twilights at one draught before night began to . . . Because, after all, this car coming from the town of Łódź and on its way to Lwów must stop. For the night. For a time when there's no spiderweb though it exists. When there's no day though it exists. When there's no God . . . although . . . And now let's turn the page of darkness. Let's open the day's eye, pretending it's we ourselves who are opening it. The jay we parted from in midair flaps wings that are a day older. The car . . . But the car's empty. Because those two, in plus fours but capless, are going down into an alder grove along a path, keeping step with a stream, only silently. Look—here's a meadow—and the young sun's already had time to put the landscape in order.

The hamlet's a long way off down there beyond junipers and some grazing heifers, all facing the same way. The young men get undressed. They're throwing their driving clothes on the grass. In no time the more sinewy of the two is exploring the shallow bottom with his heel. It's a bluish clay and is marked at once with a golden trace. Some of this water raised to their mouths—till their teeth are right on edge, their appetite so roused by this drink at an alder root.

The water's up to their knees. They're listening to it with their skin. And now they're splashing their bodies, tossing the stream onto their backs in great handfuls and letting out snorts from their young muzzles, so that the meadow actually looks around for colts . . .

What's this? A little eight-year-old cowherd who's crouched down behind some bilberries is staggered because those two over there in the brook are, as it were, blanked out. Why, there's a scent of something even here, not quite eau de cologne . . . or mandarin oranges. Their whole bodies are covered in lather from head to . . . to knees. Now the brawny one, the one more sharply nipped in at the waist, is spreading foam on the fair one's back. From the nape, right from the nape along the backbone. Now he's brought his hands to a halt at the waist. And is going up. And down. And below the waist till a yawn's overwhelming the fair one, because he's spreading his arms wide, and the other seizes the chance and soaps his armpits—and the fair one even lets his head fall backward . . . Odd, this way of soaping. Because it's only below the waist. And a sudden ticklish giggle from the fair one. What's the other one done to him? Can't see clearly from here . . .

Now it's the fair one who's soaping the athlete. And there's a flurry of hands around bodies. They rinse off till the stream flows away with a milky film. And their skin's gone pink. And they both laugh and go on splashing water at each other, only more and more brusquely. Are they going to quarrel? And now their laughter's erupting in short spurts.

The little cowherd's positively open-mouthed from looking, because these young gentlemen are up to some game! One of them tries to grab the other . . . by the hand. They're grappling with each other. They're fighting because there's a flurry of hands and things that aren't hands in this scuffle. The little cowherd's lowered his pants because all at once he wants to pee. And he looks now at them, now at his own more and more feeble trickle.

The elderly man's eye is on his watch. Then on the backdrop of the Grand'Place. Arousal of the tourist within him. To be on the old square and not trace the outlines of the gilded mansions with an enraptured eye? Right—some worn-out street map rustles in his hands. He ruffles the pages. What's he looking for? It might be an idea to help him.

"Forgive me for butting in . . . but I live here, I belong here . . . perhaps I can be of some service?" I say to him in French.

And my old man turns scarlet! The poor thing's quite confused and begins to stammer in at least three languages . . .

"*Ich* . . . *j'ai* . . . I wanted to sit here for a bit, calling odds and ends to mind . . . you know . . . the good old days . . . and I nearly dropped off . . . "

I smile, and he eyes me strangely.

"Please," he says, "sit down . . . " And he's muttered some other trivial remark, slipped in, inserted something—in what language? Italian? And has taken the lapel of his pale jacket in his hand, smiling straight in my face, half timid, half impudent.

And the conversation gets under way, forging ahead already. Yes, yes . . . certainly . . . Obviously . . . Oh, that's all over now . . . And it won't happen again . . . Clearly it won't happen. Do I belong here? Of course. And to convince this ramshackle pensioner of my belonging underpinned by the gilded Grand'Place with its sables, tigers, bananas, and blacks, I order two glasses of red wine. And the conversation continues as a foursome, these two glasses and us.

Here's what my pensioner is saying now:

"You know before the war I used to *live* . . . but now . . . " A wave of his seamed and knotted hand. He's begun to stare at me more closely:

"Excuse me, are you married?"

I cradle the wine against my palate with my tongue longer than necessary so as not to answer right away. But all the same I've got to make the effort:

"No."

He searches my face, drools over me with his pale gaze, and says:

"It's odd . . . forgive this outspokenness in someone you don't know," and his small eyes have started to take on a brighter blue again, "but with your good looks . . . Clearly you've not had the chance . . . "

"No, it's not that . . . to be perfectly frank . . . I've had chances but . . . how to put this in perspective . . . quite simply it's this way women have . . . you know . . . that cloying sweetness of theirs has always alarmed me. And then this 'routine' of theirs, everything at its proper time and in its proper place, their monthly frailties . . . "

And he nods agreement and thinks that . . . so I add hurriedly:

"Which isn't to say I'd contemplate for one moment . . . for instance . . . a liaison with some, well . . . butcher or corporal."

And he's rejuvenated! And has grown somewhat fatherly toward me. You can tell that he's controlling his mouth so as not to hurt me with adult laughter.

"I know what you mean . . . I know what you mean."

All the same, I can see that he only knows what I mean in

word, so to speak; but in his mind he's pitying me. And you can tell he's taking back something he was going to say just now. You can see how, with an exasperated tongue, he's driving back down his dark gullet words that imagined a moment ago they'd get a break, leap out, ironic, mordant, and so on . . . He's looking at me now with the eyes of a wise missus who's heard out her man's angry harangue and knows she must wait a bit, if only for the merest moment before . . .

"You're a Pole?" And he looks at me as if he's afraid I'm going to say no.

"I don't see what that's got to do with . . . yes, a Pole . . . when we're having a chat in French . . . besides, I've been here for . . . thirty years . . . so that . . . you know . . . we . . . Europeans . . . "

"Never mind, never mind . . . ," says this ramshackle man in a low voice, "but when I saw you standing at the corner, seemingly gazing at the old houses, I thought to myself: 'That fellow over there is like me. To all appearances he knows who he is, but deep down he's still caught up by his toddler's shirt on the hawthorn and bindweed, hedges and wire, . . . barbed wire . . . *Ja-ja!*' . . . "

And he's reddened, because that "*ja-ja*" of his has betrayed a Germanic shirt. Let's take our chance, since our boxer has lowered his guard:

"You're . . . German?"

This time he's gone pale. His grotesquely large fingers have started to tremble on the table (well, well, the little bird's been trapped by its talon). To hide his pallor he's drained the dregs of his wine.

"Yes . . . but from now on . . . we're going to speak Polish!"

And he looks at me, looks hard at me with those crude German forget-me-nots! And pulls himself straight on his chair! It's a miracle that the wispy relics over his ears haven't exploded in a curling cloud of fair hair. How arrogant he's grown, not to say insolent.

"Because I was born there . . . in the town of Łódź. Ah, my dear man, what a town that was!"

"Litzmanstadt," I toss at him, offhand. He darts me a glance, not so much of reproach as of regret to see that after thirty years I'm still gritting unsound teeth . . . But it's as if he's beginning to smile with relief as well because at last we're in the trenches. Leaping as we run we've crossed Europe, and by now each of us is seated in his own dugout, waiting. With a bayonet . . . One glance at me and he lowers his eyes for a fraction of a second, then raises them again . . .

because he's looking at the peasant woman who's putting a bowl of curds in front of those two young men fresh from bathing in the water in the middle of the meadow . . . and who's saying, "The spuds'll be ready soon. . . ," and he sees a dish of new, almost too new potatoes shining with butter! And sees Hans's jaws at work and Hans's spoon now on the plate, now in his blowing mouth . . . And hears the downpour that's deluging from a sultry sky and must be walloping into their car over there on the road and—let him hear them there as well . . .

here, too, here among the gilded mansions . . .

let him hear the last thunderclaps scattering the black sky to the four winds, a sky from which suddenly naked sun is being poured in buckets. And there they both are on the doorstep—and the farmer's wife's saying: "Away with you! I won't have no cash for food . . . " So the fair one slips something into the hand of the child who's trying to count the wheels on their car, and the lad takes to his heels, rushing to the kitchen . . . They pass beehives. The small roofs are steaming from their dark shingles. And on the greenery, so many glistenings and silverings, so many gleams, all over spittle from the firm little tongues of angels . . . And the throat positively itches because of the bees' venom. Bees have swarmed right across the front of one hive, turning the surface russet, so that the actual orifice can only be guessed at by the swirl of their influx. And balsam pulses from that hole.

The young men stop because their throats are full of this coarse-grained air; they stop because they can't wrench their eyes from this press of bees that penetrates and withdraws, set agog by the storm that is still—look there! above the forest!—striking flints for heavenly muskets. They look at each other till a smile starts to curl itself round their lips. And already Hans is inserting the starting handle . . .

"Maybe we could go . . . there's a small square a couple of hundred yards away, so many cars here," I say, because we've been silent for some time, waiting for the May tourists to pass us on their leisurely rounds.

He's a little out of breath. So it's a relief for him to sit down again. He hasn't forgotten his huge fingers. He's arranged them on his knees. Now he's picked them up again as if trying for a better place. All this time our shoes are exploring the gravel that has paled to the color on turtledoves' breasts. And the shoes can't see the end of the little path that gets lost in the geometry of flowerbeds marked out by spherical myrtle and a circular pool. His vast shoes are so flabby and worn that even polish doesn't make any difference. The nanny opposite on a bench under the half-shade of a plane tree keeps one eye on a brat, over the top of a weekly bloated with pop stars. But now she's had a look at these old blighters. She's looking at us.

"What language are they into? You can't grab a word. A way-out lingo. Hey—now the one with thick gropers is starting to shake his head around. He's shaking it and keeps shaking it real cool. And the other" (the "other" in question is me) "tarted up round his gray fluff, he's fined the fingers of both hands down, and with those rocketing sticks, those brushes, he's holding his own against the German's vocals."

"Maaaybe, but life didn't treat you so badly over there . . . And now with a modest pension . . . you can still travel and so . . ."

The other knots and unknots his huge fingers, but up above it's as if he's fallen into a dream, falling into the past like a student into a hayrick behind which a girl's hiding, sweating with summer. He frames words with his lips but his eyes are still far away, no doubt among harvestings, tresses of hair, dews on hay. God knows what. Now he's talking:

"My dear man . . . life didn't do anything to me there . . . not there or later in Paris . . . I *lived* . . . " (and he sees that I want to add something) "wait . . . I . . . you know . . . every day *I wanted to live!* Very much so!"

"All the same you *are* living now . . . only now you've gotten away from your job."

And the German's broken out with a twenty-year-old's laugh!

"My dear man, I . . . I never had a job in my life! My father tried to get me interested in the factory . . . he paid for my studies in Switzerland . . . and I . . . "

And you can see that his eyes can't cope with the assault of dream landscapes that storm his front from behind the lines in a rainbowed brigade.

"You aren't going to tell me" (his audacity is quite shocking at his advanced age) " . . . you're not going to tell me that right up to this day . . . you've lived alone, without family, without any . . . "

"Don't lose yourself in suppositions. Never alone . . . that's for sure. And in point of fact—it's simple. Ever since my school days only one thing's mattered: boys."

Well, he's pretty well knocked me off my stride with this! I've smiled, but I'm not my own man. I've screwed up my eyes and put my palms on my knees, more or less miming the formula, "Well . . . tastes differ." All the same, I know that some sort of reply is needed, so I reply:

"Well, of course . . . these things happen . . . and viewing the matter statistically . . . Well, and literature's full of examples . . . " (the German is nodding his head). "But aren't you exaggerating . . . when you define your whole life . . . by this thing? You know . . . as man's entire destiny? There are values after all" (I'm being all but ironic) "that mankind passes down . . . Even you, though you've retired, you can still . . . "

The pensioner raises a hand, wanting to interrupt. And he does interrupt:

"I can, I can . . . do you know what I can do as a pensioner? I can sit myself down in a park on a bench, and when a squirrel runs up to me, give it nuts, taking my dentures out of my mouth in the meantime and cleaning them with a toothpick. I can do that much. And you" (he's looking at my hair), "can you really still do that much?"

I smile at all events, but he can see that it's a dialectical smile. However, he doesn't let me know this.

"What can I do? You know . . . I feel quite simply that I'm a member of society in the full sense . . . in teaching . . . I try to keep faith with certain principles which for centuries . . . have been handed down from generation to generation."

And the German positively leaps up. So that the nanny opposite, who's been absorbed in her reading, lowers her weekly and glances at the child in its carriage because that man's whirling his arms and he's got the kind of arms that set the air trembling . . .

"My good sir! What's this that's 'been handed down from generation to generation'? 'Thou shalt love thy neighbor as thyself' no doubt? Society?! Rogues and sycophants always to the fore! And knowledge—good for riffling through rancid encyclopedias and filling up more petty sheets of paper and making petty piles of them . . . to add new molds to old!" (He's going at it with a will!) "What the hell will anyone get out of this! What the hell will anyone get out of the fact that Professor So-and-so starts counting . . . how should I know? . . . all those women in Goethe's bed . . . or . . . the uses of the genitive singular?! But my good sir, what's that got to do with a man of flesh and blood, with you, with me?!" (He's looking at me and has pale periwinkle in his eyes, waist-high.) "Do you know what counts? Joy . . . pleasure . . . to . . . dilate in a flash, as if a good half-dozen lungs inside you are starting to breathe frosty air . . . as if . . . "

. . . woodpeckers were hammering with their beaks. They hammer and prod. How many are there? Bark scatters on the snow. In the firebreaks the snow is so powdery that this forest's crying out for Christmas Eve hunting. We'll pause in our writing for a moment. We'll put aside the heated ballpoint, because something must happen under such a sky in answer to our hope. Look there! Look over there! A sleigh's approaching already—and a second—and a fifth. Bristling with shotguns and filled with sheepskins. They glide along making grasses crackle and frostbitten greenery squeal. They get out, and only their noses emerge from their sheepskin coats. And there's a lot of puffing and rubbing of hands. And now the gamekeeper's placing them skillfully. But on tiptoe without a word . . . Shots, one, two, and three. From woods worlds away. That's the signal for the drive. For peasants to hollo through the forest, driving a troop of maddened hares in front of them. Now. Very close. Look, they're here already! Now, from behind an alder hoarfrosted to bone, something small makes a dash. And shotguns to shoulders. Look, here's a second! A mass of them! With Christian shot the hunters riddle the eyes of those hares . . . who, faithful to tradition, will wake up the day after tomorrow in Christmas pies.

It's all over. The hunters swig tea from their thermoses, tea so strong that an infant would carol lustily after it! And one of the faces is flushed by drinking, and the eyes—the reader's guessed by now who our subject is and that those eyes are the color of periwinkle . . . Even before all the tea's been drunk, the first hint of evening in the forest air. Then the sleighs make a half-turn, the runners find their tracks again and go skimming along the firebreak, through osier stubble onto fields, across fields—and to the manor house! The landowner, a confirmed bachelor, has invited these hunting gentry here.

Strange hunters . . . They don't even notice how many hares there are. They stamp their boots, struggle out of their sheepskins. Nothing but straightening of sweaters, combing of thick hair, viewing themselves in mirrors . . . And the mirrors are astounded as they're still replete with curls, shoulder straps, décolletées cut low to the nipple with a little fichu lure that's tossed aloft, and in a flash a cavalier—up he goes! But here are these male langors. And at the same time a sporting stylishness and a clinking of glasses against the background of a fire of birch logs, gray no longer, till there's a spurt right to the ceiling of that golden vodka which makes men feel brotherly and intimate.

Look—wide-open doors. In breeches so tight that it's a miracle buttons don't pop off in boorish fashion straight at the mirrors—waiters with trays. Ah, these are the beaters still giving off the smell of that sweating, chase, and holloing. On the trays smoked meats, horseradish, mustard, eggs, and fresh glasses . . . Without a pause this stalwart . . . scoops up horseradish on a slice of sausage and stuffs his mouth . . . says something to his companion through horseradish and vodka . . . The other breaks out into such a laugh that the mirrors exchange glances . . . No, it must be a mistake . . . it's the one standing with Thomas who's laughed like that.

They make the rounds with the trays somewhat ponderously, all boots, these bogus waiters whose mugs smell of stable straw. Time and again they toss their hair back from their foreheads, and more and more merrily because of the vodka, so much do the gentlemen from town drink with them and to them.

And now the host winds up the gramophone with a slightly tipsy hand . . . and at once this hand's grabbed by a purple cavalry captain! The hunters dance. Couple after couple. The waiters are a part of the dance. Boots gleam, iron heels on boards, till the town-dwellers' hair looks as if it was trying to fall about their shoulders but can't . . . till the town-dwellers are nothing but quickened breathing, sighing, half-closing eyes . . . Even the mirrors take umbrage—as they have to reflect these sweat-soaked backs for you (because sweaters have vanished!), these tight breeches, this stylishness of the stable, this forbidden ball . . . which squeezes in on itself and sweats and staggers with the dance . . . toward the staircase whose handrail . . .

A strange beast, the handrail. Not marble, sleek as a plump matron's thigh, but the ruddy pitch-pine kind polished to amber like the shoulder of some fifteen-year-old boy when he runs out of a river.

Now, or rather then, or rather at the moment when all those hares and bogus waiters and Thomas with his fair curls and the purple cavalry captain . . . Why purple? A mass of hands on the resinous handrail now. They're going upstairs. Small rooms here, their ceilings stained with damp . . . and this . . . and now better not to speak of it. Because when the ploughboy's turned the lamp up a bit, everything's glowing nut-brown, it's true, but above the bed the wall's so cracked that you can see brickwork here and there where plaster's come adrift. We can see it from here, we who are thinking about it, as if we were standing there now, looking around at the walls and throwing off threads because this little stove's warmed up so they're stark naked. The mahogany looks at those rough peasant trousers thrown down anyhow and at these metropolitan plus fours right next to the trousers. And the people in photographs have actually raised their heads and pretend to be searching for something on the ceiling so as not to contemplate this messy dress, rumpus, and chase. And the lamp seems as if it were on their side, because it smokes, dies down, so that you won't recognize who's on top in this scuffle, whose hair is dark, and whose . . . On the other side of the wall as well, trampling, bumping into furniture. And on the stairs a rumbling sound. But for some reason no one's laughing. Ah! Now someone's cried out, but it's as if this voice has rebounded off the floor and set up a whine like a dog's. Mmm . . . from behind this door nothing but breathing, but such breathing that one moment door and windows have curved in, then they've curved out. And even the house moves in time to this panting, even the frost-flowers twist themselves into brutish graffiti in time to cries of "To hell with you . . . plane it, push, go the whole hog you brute! . . . "

"My dear man . . . "—and he digs at the gravel with his shoe and looks at me with that impudently twinkling eye of his—"how can I give a clear idea here about how it was then" (he grabs his entire cheek in his hand!), "and how can this ramshackle muzzle emit words that in any case won't convey what I was up to in that room. He didn't even want to, to start with . . . he was scared. He was scared of sin, though the landowner slipped them two złotys each . . . well, and that vodka did its . . . so he gave in." (He laughs to himself as he looks at that scuffle with the struggling quasi-waiter.) "Ah, my dear man . . . that stink of sweat on a body you don't know, muscles . . . you can smile . . . muscles without ladies' lard, so that it's all tendons and just like a lumber-yard, hacking and hewing away . . . And then you know, when I was reaching the end of my task, Olek squirted over those family photographs, the horse boy, over those white ladies at watering places, over those children with little baskets for scattering flowers beneath the priest's feet, over those landowners with curved sabers—so it ran down the masters' walls . . . then . . . in that manor ridden down by a snowstorm on the backs of a hundred devils!"

And he pulled off a triumphant grimace. Then my turn, though my face held no smile:

"Two hunts . . . the first for pies and the second with two-złoty pieces for farmhands running in stark snow. To blaze away at them from raised barrels, from your gentry's double-barreled guns . . . "

And old Thomas, whose sleek layers of mature bark the woodpeckers have hacked off, rootling his muzzle into a gray mask—he obviously remembers something because his mouth twists in mockery:

"And you . . . please forgive this impertinence . . . has it only been women who've attracted you?"

I keep quiet because I don't even know if I should go through the motions of reflecting . . . And he takes my head in his gargantuan fingers and shakes it until its gray hairs start to sough, to surge in waves and billow crazily as if back-combed by a wind, a dark-haired tanned wind from forty calendars ago, which used to swing the Carpathian firs like bells.

And as he's shaking my head like this, a bottle falls out from behind my ear, from under my brows . . . and is growing close to my head, brought to birth by me, made of green glass . . . And he takes this newborn thing between his shovel palms . . . "With all due respect, this is yours . . . ," and Thomas gives me this bottle, and inside is fat Anielka, boozed up and bruised by soldiers, sprawling and snoring. What about this forfeit I'm holding in my fingers, what about this vessel with its cargo of need and short commons under the colors of love . . . And the German takes me by the arm as if I were an invalid and the bottle falls to the ground right there. And no glass, no Anielka, only a fistful of bruises on the gravel. No one here will pick them up . . . On the other hand, I've got dark hair. Auburn, tending to dark. And now I'm singing, certainly a hymn, as I'm agape, I'm closing my eyes, I'm hot, I'm unbuttoning the neck of my shirt, as there's a crush in the church portico that— Christ! and in front of me is Janka, the one they call stupid, and I'm praying up against her, but I don't dare with my hand because . . . And I only sense that . . . and here's the censer from the altar. And here from under Janka's armpits, from under . . . And I'm opening my eyes and everyone's opened their eyes, . . . and we all close them again, the better to "Mother of God, Star of the sea, Pray for the wanderer, Pray for me" . . . and I only sense that Janka's leaning on me—aah! it's happened. And furtively I squirm toward the door with my maculate unhappy hand in my pocket. The German goes with me. He can see that impudent hand and that flight from the sullied Maytime church. And he looks at my head, which is gradually starting to seek out colors not in oak bark but in slops.

It's true that the sung words are still circling round about in the air, clipped out by the rosy pastry cutters of women's mouths in that stifling Marian fug over there.

But here—the nanny gets to her feet, smooths down her crumpled skirt, and sails off with the brat. And in no time a sociological sparrow's settled on the bench to check up on his conjectures in the field of economics.

Importunate and predominant presence of sex thanks to this old man. And the fellow doesn't even make excuses for himself. Just ruminates on his cute little flowers-in-spring right there in front of me. Not a cow. A ruminating bull. Two bulls. Bull on bull. What he's imagining to himself.

"And . . . where did you spend the war . . . if one may ask?"

The German's grown more cheerful.

"Oh, nothing of interest . . . you know . . . I stayed in Łódź as long as I could, and you know . . . often met up with . . . soldiers coming from or to the front . . . we had a sort of café . . . Toward the end I had to take some kind of job just for window dressing . . . I was a kind of overseer for landed estates . . . "

"You went on . . . hunting?"

"I went on . . . hunting . . . And when the Germans came looking for partisans, I'd say: 'Partisans? Here?' They'd take a German at his word . . . " And he laughs, pleased with . . . "And you know, I didn't have to put on a uniform till three months before the capitulation . . . to make it harder to run away . . . and still harder to get back . . . scraping a living here . . . among foreigners . . . balls!"

Everything's topsy-turvy in my mind. I was just thinking

I'd pin this vast black, yellow, and red butterfly down, and now the colors have scattered off its wings. Any minute . . . the next thing will be . . . it's he who's the patriot! Hang on! Casually, I'm taking off my jacket—as if I'm hot. I put it on the bench beside me and start rolling up my sleeve. Once, twice, three times. And on my forearm: 46 333.

And I can see that he's looking. That he knows he must look. Now he starts nodding his head compassionately:

"My dear man . . . what's to be said to THAT? It's a kind of holy mange . . . you don't know whether to wipe it away or put it in a little frame and stop living and do nothing but light a candle in front of it . . . That's why I've never liked looking at cripples . . . "

But I'm not one to give way at once . . . what does he think? That I'm going to roll down my sleeve, do up my button, and the show's over? I thrust this number right under his gaze. And he sees these corpselike figures advancing on his baggy eyes, sees that I'm driving these gray geese up to his muzzle, that the Brussels sky is donning stripes, striped prison garments, and that with my left foot I'm treading on his pensioner's shoe . . . The next minute he's tearing open his shirt with his huge fingers and baring the collapsed chest of a desiccated mushroom. And on this chest some sort of Afro-Asio-design! Tattooed in violet and livid green. Not quite minarets, not quite pricks roused by a spring wind, as so much of it is dancing projection and bamboo parallels. And above all this, two eyes the color of dolly-blue. While below, the beginning of an inscription running down over the belly.

And this arrogant German stands in front of me just so, like some old bum paid to lug a sandwich board through the streets billing the dirty program for This Very Night!

But voices. Voices of office workers strolling this way along the paths toward the Gare Centrale. Soft crunch of their shoes on the gravel. They see two elderly gentlemen busily doing up their buttons. They see the elegant one making sweeping gestures. Then see them going in the direction of the parking lot. And now no one can see them. Because we're in my car.

Why did I invite him to lunch? Let's leave that to future generations, who in any case are going to mix everything up and apply their own fantasies to the period under scrutiny. To hell with them. I invited him on the day when American robot think tanks started to pillage the memory of Mars . . . I invited him because I was hungry, of course . . . No. Because his senile cheeriness exasperated me, that healthily animal delight of his, the whole of his world whose peaks were overgrown with pubic hair.

The waiter stood over us, smiling through the frame of his dark gray mustache, which made him look like a veteran of twenty years' service. We ordered a salad with roquefort and nuts, followed by a steak "à la Unicorn."

We're eating, putting on amicable airs, emitting daisy-chain words, bouquets of phrases through mouthfuls of rustic cheese salad. I'm there with him, but I'm constantly thinking about the Arabian design inscribed in Indian ink and colors on his belly forty years ago. And he's champing away and staggering across the table with those huge fingers, sometimes even banging against a plate with his great ring. But he seems calm. I pour more wine. So as to spellbind both him and myself with youth because then maybe our tattoos . . . what? I don't know myself . . . and he looks at me and senses that my hostility and aggression have waned and are still waning. And I keep on thinking about his tattoo. I'll take him from the flank.

"In the concentration camps," I say, licking lemon mousse off a little spoon, "I used to see fellows with tattoos . . . not politicals, that's for sure . . . oh . . . judging by the area of the designs you could pretty well work out the criminal records of the little rascals . . . One of them had . . . tattooed on his back . . . you know . . . a ginger cat. And this cat was chasing a pearly gray mouse half-hidden . . . guess where!"

"Ha-ha-haaaaa!" Thomas explodes with laughter so that customers at other tables actually turn around to look at us for a second. "Sure I can guess where . . . but you see . . . what they've done to you . . . mother, school, and priests! Instead of saying the mouse is running up his arse . . . you wrap it up in euphemisms, in stutterings" (he's getting more serious), "but as for . . . as for these tattoos . . . it's quite obvious you still haven't got the idea . . . "

We had coffee at my place.

" . . . when I showed you that design on my belly back there . . . in the sun . . . you looked at it as if you were seeing jailbird filth . . . my good sir, that was LOVE!"

He stood up, trembling so much that he actually had to lean a hand on the wall, and began to unbutton his shirt. Look, now he's pulling it out of his trousers. Now look, he's undone all its buttons. And he's unbuttoning his pants. And lowering them like at a doctor's. And on his belly, in letters livid with age, is written YAZIT. And that wrinkled belly starts to stammer at me while he holds his beggarly pensioner's shirt spread out like wings. This ramshackle windbag's looking at me as well and says:

"Now then read my good sir! For him and only for him I had myself tattooed, for that fourteen-year-old Berber with blue eyes, damn it, now then read my good sir!"

"Yazit . . . ," I read out.

"Yazit . . . Yazit . . . Yazit . . . "

Yazit's eyes, blue as dolly-blue stirred by night, were boring into me. I lowered my own.

You've scarcely raised your eyes from the point where I lowered mine and once again you're plunging into a sentence. Because cheek by jowl we're riding bareback on words that transport us into a work scarcely apprehended but already clearly penned along two contending currents condemned to brotherhood.

Day and night unravel from the selfsame eyeballs; a

stream that bears both the sun to the deeps and the sleep, the dreams of every creature that breathes. On the left the raven sent out each day through darkness, on the right the dove, native of . . .

And words, still piled in a heap, wait for the hand that will thrust in among them, seeking out its own. Just here are the figures fashioned yesterday. Look—here. Let them be assembled here. Let the episodic jay perch here, the wrinkled Thomas next in line. Let him launch toward us with his huge paw the peasant woman and those two *"Schöns,"* the Pole from the gilded Grand'Place and himself, that moldering creature who once upon a time in his youth used to stuff himself with night and now spits it out through black-holed stars . . .

Or maybe only wake up the rascal jay and wipe out the world with its wing so that sky alone would remain . . . Because then it will be enough to clap your hands and raise some rusty file of snipe from the marshes so that there can be a narrative line in the sky about the third season of the year. And now that we already have a firmament with an infallible sign, let's put a *Station* under it. The rest will follow from this assumption. A train will start to hover eagerly, porters will hump suitcases, and that lady over there by the wall will all of a sudden spread her downy furs wide at the sight of an adolescent schoolboy and there—only her, whitely naked under the fur coat! And her black crow. And there she is, whispering something with her poppy-red lips and wrapped up once more, wrapped round, a countess from suburban Hajnowka, accounted yours for a złoty.

Now from left to right, like mist or locomotive steam. Whoever's in its embrace is a passenger. Wave to him with something white and very soon he'll start to sigh, blot a tear in his left eye, just above the heart . . . there's the magic of this place for you.

By this time there are violet lights on the facade. By this time up to three hundred leaves are tearing themselves from nearby maples and flying off. In no time they're striking against the station clock. Look . . . now they're fluttering down the length of the wall, disorderly, cavorting like goats, floating like angels. Only we are watching them from here through so many translucent years . . . They were waiting for this moment there, in a mysterious limbo, just so that I'd name them today, bring them from somewhere or other into the Warsaw air, provincial leaves, my mantle against the winter of stony czardoms.

Now they're falling at people's feet. They even fawn on booted legs brazen with polish, on that fellow straddling, hands in breeches. And two others with him. Now they go into the hall . . . That . . . That's presumably Olek, because those two behind him, like military and secular acolytes at a Corpus Christi festival, are supporting him by the elbows.

A smell's drifted from somewhere, of eau de cologne under armpits, raspberry juice with garlic . . . Aaaah . . . because here where they've stopped, the door to the station urinals is open. *Gents.* Sure, gents go to and fro. Look, a man with a limp coming out—well, well . . . Look, a fellow with a tan briefcase and a maladroit hand finishing doing up his fly, where there's a flash of dark blue shirt. And, quick, on to the platform!

And those three have pushed their caps to the backs of their heads and are watching this hurly-burly of humanity, this scurrying, scattering slagheap with luggage that they put down, shift from left hand to right or from right to left— hurry up!—because the loudspeaker's making some announcement.

All at once Olek's adjutant acolytes grab him—whoa!— by the elbows. And their faces are at the ready. Because an elegant man's come into the hall. He's come to a halt and started to view the hall in a leisurely fashion. No doubt the station's a museum to him, as he's looking along walls that are simply asking for a Sicilian *Primavera.* Why, he's even looking up for pennies from the station's heaven.

But anyone who could see his nose would notice restive nostrils. Because this young man in his slim-fitting autumn coat and fawn hat on a fair head of hair has already flared the scent issuing in a spicy ribbon from the urinals by the exit into the square where the maples are sprinkling their leaves.

By this time the young man's caught on to the smiles of the three men over there by the fountain for Gents. And so he lights a cigarette and forward!—to the source of the stream.

"You know . . . at that time I'd . . . oh . . . well . . . I was a whelp. And this was my first sortie after the ones who walk the streets . . . for cash . . . and what's more in Warsaw. At home in Łódź I'd never have dared . . . Only instead of wearing something . . . well, to do it on a dirty bench in the park, I'd dressed myself up as if I was off to the Riviera! And when I went into the hall I saw them at once."

"'Them' . . . you mean they had some sort of trademark?"

"They were standing by the urinals . . . in the casual kind of way you'd stand on . . . on a seafront, leaning on railings and watching for a three-master from Indonesia . . . Take the plunge? And you know . . . all at once I've smelled the station smell. So I go toward them. But I've taken fright. I veer off toward the Gents. And I can feel they're following me with their eyes. And by now I'm starting to regret that . . . but by this time they're standing next to me on either side. And those breeches of theirs facing front, spines bent back. And the idea is we're pissing."

And he goes on telling me more details about them and about his blushing self as he then was, and I've plastered up a smile of the "yes, yes, that's riveting" type—but I'm not there because I'm standing in the basement of the Gare Saint-Lazare in front of a green wall and I'm pissing along with the others, spitting and pissing into that stream at my feet . . . I glance at my neighbor, and he's tossing his meat in the hollow of his hand, a covert eye on whether I can see . . .

I look to the left and a soldier's there, not even young, weighing his pound of pink ham on his palm. And there's a fish-market smell . . .

And I hear Thomas speaking louder and louder, so I nod with a head that's still Paris-based and increase my smile by one size, implying that of course . . . I'm still running after his sentences like a dog without shifting my snitch from the shaggy scent.

" . . . And Olek says, 'Well how about it? Shall we go?' And you know . . . his hand's already making free with me . . . 'Yes,' I say, and add, 'OK by me . . . ' But at the same time delight and terror are jostling in my heart . . . The hall had to be crossed. Together. Olek wants it at his place. Says it's not too far away. And you know, I was in a funk, who knows what sort of fellow he . . . so I say I'd rather in the park. And he laughs: 'All on the fresh green grass oh!' . . . And tells me the price, I don't remember how much anymore.

"Through streets. Today I can't even recall whether it was the beginnings of a park or a little square with a few benches and rhododendron clumps. He's glanced around to make sure no police are about—and hup! he shoves me into the bushes."

He's gone quiet for a moment.

" . . . Where is he now, Olek? After . . . forty years . . . My dear man . . . after forty years. Is he alive? And even if . . . " (he's let out a sigh, smiling ruefully) "he's just the same sort of old chap as me! Decaying, ripe for the rubbish dump."

He's gotten up. As if wanting by getting up to summon all his body's energy. And he's grinned in a young, even jeering way.

" . . . My dear man . . . maybe today I'd not be scared of kneeling down on that overcoat . . . arse bare to the September wind—but . . . him . . . I'd be scared of Olek today."

And my German takes me by the arm, and on that May afternoon, this tourist I invited to coffee points out through my window where he was kneeling in my garden, where the benches were that he could see from his kneeling position, where the old woman was standing wrapped in a plaid, her dog turning in circles because it couldn't find the ideal spot . . . At last he's got it. "And at the very same moment Olek has me . . . My dear man, I don't know how I survived it, how he didn't succeed in chiseling me to death there . . . "

He's let out a sigh. He's fixed his gaze on a flowerbed overgrown with Saint-John's-wort that's already put out tiny heads of buds and is only waiting for Saint John's Midsummer Day sign to explode with new light. And this guest of mine stands like this, denying his today. Now he's slowly turning his head toward me. But his face is smooth! Not a single wrinkle! His nose thrusts at the world and his eyes exult over that brutish night's work of forty years ago. He's looking at me.

"You're still young . . . You could . . . "

The next day after breakfast I went with him to the Musée des Beaux Arts. Not all pictures like you to go up to them. The ones of the court, of Serene Highnesses, yes, by all means, because power's portrayed in them, gleams of weapons and blood are enough to scare you off, just as the ones of merchants like a tourist to look at them, at that good wife who's removed her hands from cod and hellish big eels to sit posing against a background of marble and a sailing ship. I get my information from the pictures themselves.

"While there are no gawkers we gaze at ourselves. And we don't need the sun or pages torn off a calendar. We call out to each other, we jabber inanities cunningly packed in proverbs. And when it's not too hot—we amuse ourselves with a guessing game: 'Who said this?' Everyone in these pictures, two hundred and sixty-eight of us, personages and creatures. The Hieronymus-Boschers close their eyes. Then we, the Breughlers, let out a word . . . or something else as well . . . and we call out: 'Who's that?' And they guess:

"It's a . . . bell farting on a bass note . . .

"It's a . . . spire ripping open the big bellies of storks . . .

"It's a . . . confessor who's already thrust half his snout into an arse

and is raking out sin with his tongue . . .

"No! It's an egg, an egg, an egg full of the world,

waiting for a purple beak . . .

"It's a . . . stinking shaggy crown

with salty grief dripping from it . . .

"It's easy for the Hieronymus-Boschers to do imitations, because nearly all of them have their mouths open as if they laid eggs not from behind but from their snouts . . .

"Don't be cocky—just for that, you've got to kiss Icarus on the heel . . . You all, wrapped up in your old furs, coated by tinsmiths with metal foil just like Easter bunnies, fit to make the enemy split his sides laughing!

"And you all then . . .

"Shhh . . . gawkers coming!"

"You know . . . in the entire building . . . it's really this corner that counts. Everywhere else it's . . . grub in the raw: poultry, game, fish as big as kneading troughs . . . on the whole just so much meat ripe for slaughter or fucking . . . but here it's something else."

Thomas is smiling.

"I see you want to dose me with culture and get me away from 'meat' by preventive medicine . . . To cure the past?"

"Ooooh . . . I think *so wie so* the case is doomed to failure. All the same . . . before you leave I'd like you to get to know this humanity of Bosch's, painted with such fidelity . . . because it's metaphysical . . . thanks to the indiscretion of some agnostic devils."

Thomas bursts out laughing.

"Not only devils. Look here. And heeere . . . "

I looked along his finger. Objects and people entering each other recklessly. With body, weapons, and every kind of sharp instrument they possess. But here, to my ears, this laugh of Thomas's smacked somehow of the stable. And somehow in this laugh of his that he'd grafted fulsomely on certain scenes in the picture, Olek came alive for me.

"That . . . Olek . . . did you ever meet him again?"

And Thomas had just pointed a finger aimed at the kind of little scene he relished when he heard my question. He drew back his hand, let it fall, and looked at me like the time he felt impelled to show me the tattoo on his belly.

"We loved each other for twelve years, Olek and I."

He stretched out his hand again, but because we were moving along, we'd passed those bodies yoked in bliss, so that his huge fingers were pointing instead to a city on fire at night and were actually glowing red in the light of this drama, irrelevantly indicated.

" . . . twelve years if you please . . . "

It sounded like a parody, unintended and so unsuccessful.

" . . . Does it strike you as funny?"

"Whyyy—not at all!" I replied. "Every way of keeping faith . . . or even . . . well . . . in this earthly chaos of ours order deserves esteem."

And Thomas bursts out laughing for the second time. What could I have said to make him laugh? Because it was perfectly obvious. He hadn't invented his laugh just like that, extempore. He'd been forced to laugh at my words.

"Get away with your 'keeping faith' . . . We suited each other. That's all . . . my dear man, that's a lot!"

Suddenly I saw them both there in the park, holding each other by the hand, and furtively evading whiplash snow cutting at their muzzles.

"Didn't winter put a stop to your . . . well . . . those get-togethers?"

"I hired a room. He used to come to me . . . 'keeping faith' . . . hang on . . . listen . . . it was a Sunday. I'm expecting him, but for some reason he doesn't show up. At last he comes. 'He didn't want to let me go!' he says, because you know, he was going with a sergeant too, like a battering ram, not a man! You know, he was going with him before we got together. 'He didn't want to let me go, and I've dashed straight from his place,' says Olek. And this rouses me, and I say to him: 'So then you're still piping hot from your corporal' (I always used to joke that it was a corporal, not a sergeant), 'get your clothes off!'

"And he's kind of disconcerted. And so he says:

"'Hang on, I just—' 'No,' I say, and grab him by the arm, 'you're not off anywhere,' because I'd guessed at once what was up . . . He looks into my eyes and smiles, but uneasily . . . So I say to him, 'Lie down!' You'll have guessed that the corporal had smeared him up to the shoulders with vanilla!"

"Sergeant . . ."

"That's right, sergeant . . ."

A family's coming out of the Rubens room: young parents, thirtyish, small daughter and son of just the right age. They look around. The mother points out Icarus. They approach piously and look him in the heel.

" . . . because I don't feel any disgust" (he's lowered his voice) " . . . you know . . . Olek knew I could *hear* that . . . soldier inside him . . . And then when it was . . . over . . . he asks if I'm not angry about it.

"'I like it,' I say. 'I like to thrust myself into someone else's bliss!'

"And he's in fits. And kisses me on the mouth with all his might and says, 'I like you, lad, because you're such a swine like me!'"

He's gone quiet. The parquet's begun to creak. Someone goes past us, obviously a tourist, chubby-cheeked in trousers just a trifle too short. Thomas has come to a halt. I've paused as well. He's looked at me and read in my face not so much disgust as bemused shock, a kind of disoriented stupefaction, a stupefaction that's broken loose from its dictionary definition and drifted into silence along with choked-back insults.

But no. It's essential the fellow should hear in this place, in the presence of these pictures, my considered opinion. Besides I *must* lodge a protest as a halberdier's leaning out and eyeing me, that peasant's craning his unshaven chops in my direction and eyeing me, that mother of slaughtered innocents has her eye on me, too. Speak! I speak.

"I could quite understand your trip to the station . . . A youngster lacking confidence, from a good family . . . wants to tear his new Sunday clothes on a nail, as it were . . . He goes where the sort who recruit for a dangerous voyage are on the prowl . . . Oh, I know what you mean, it was the time of year for that . . . We both remember those leaves that tore themselves off the maples and went spiraling . . . Well then, you wanted to get free of the civilized world, too, away from a cold continent to islands that swim in warm seas . . . The station helped you to push off from the everyday . . . When all's said we differ, you and I, as to the price we put on this gesture, but that's another matter . . . And on this impulse, you transgressed another city limit . . . But I repeat, you went with the *intention* of trespassing . . . Well, and what did you do . . . with that three-master? You anchored it alongside . . . a Warsaw backyard meant for washerwomen to dry their dirty linen on poles. Because what else was it, joining a corporation . . . the sergeant, you and no doubt others . . . exploiting that . . . well . . . Olek!"

Thomas's head jerked up. There were upheavals under his jowls. He didn't exactly want to belch invective or ejaculate a pitying word. But for a moment a group of Americans dressed in yellow and pistachio drove us apart. When they'd gone past it had grown quiet. Without willing it, we looked at a picture. And there, from December elms, rooks had taken to the air. And crows. And circle, minuscule above the parquet, knee-high to a child in preschool. And try out a flapping sound. And widening circles. And by this time are circling above us. And over that distant station and park, so that all of a sudden we've begun to feel small and sightless,

---

floundering into that snow under a sky of birds black as the brow of death.

Well, what then? My adversary's flagged and stands drooping like some nature-study teacher who, when he notices March 21 on the calendar, hurries to his herbarium and pulls out gladioli ruined by overlong storage, covered with pink mold, and tries to plant them right by the photo of his military service days. But just then it tumbles over, a corm crumbles . . . aaah . . . aaah . . . the old naturalist sneezes. And so much for his ringing of resurrection bells.

He plays the philosopher. Instead of waving a hand from the coach, like the rest of the white-downed senior German citizens, he took leave of me shaking his head sagely, lost in thought maybe, or maybe just "Eh, what a life . . . "

In August, it's like this: clouds piled in the sky sprinkled with gunpowder all set for a storm! On earth the same thing: the Italian ice-cream man piles up helpings till they teeter under a foaming mane of whipped cream.

My acquaintances have flown off to far-flung countries to take a good look at cockfights among tastefully starved children, not to mention seances with Hindu gurus of the soul who'll swallow a snake for you while you wait and pull it out of a cow's arse in a trice, made more perfect by a thousand incarnations.

At the Gare du Midi there are groups of bivouacking tourists, groups of tourists in line like geese along the wall with red-hot posies of fries. Take care to sidestep those scattered legs so as to reach the brochures by the wall over there. A bit further, porcelain tiles. Deserted here, only a dignified lady presiding over the spring, annihilating the faintest of mini-smells with chloride, chloride, chloride. But alongside the platform an engine, gasping asthmatically. A birch-twig broom shuffles and scrapes, helping butts and paper scraps to hop on the current and sail the gutter swollen now with fast-flowing water. Granite edge of pavement spattered by the mechanical motion of birch-broom bristles topped off by a Senegalese. Parisian birch tree. And its bole? And its bark? To flames and ash.

And again we're confronted by Thomas's face. And confronted by his first letter.

When he was in Brussels—it was as if hard facts count, away with romanticizing and sentiment . . . But in his letter the fellow adopts the style of Oscar Wilde, "shares with me" various so-called "thoughts" . . . why, even gives me advice . . . If it weren't for him I wouldn't have known to this day that I was living "a communal, humdrum life, taking pride in my ordinariness" . . . And he . . . that dehydrated horse-radish trying to retrieve its first flavor! He urges me to "seek out real life," "self-oriented, fleshed-out life." And wants me to make a start in Paris.

Enclosed, a map of "free men's alley" with addresses of "hot spots." He's drawn it up especially for me, based on a certain species of newssheet. It goes without saying I haven't brought it with me. So I'm in Paris on my own terms. I drink a small cup of café crème and revel in croissants at Les Deux Magots. This is a chapel where box pews are polished by the trousers and skirts of homegrown and foreign snobs.

Tourists on the pavement. Take photos of them and they'll grow old on the spot, to be viewed like the dead on a corpselike print or "projected" into quasi-life on a starched shroud. But like this for the time being, part of Now. They notice me and are already fixing my russet croissants in their brainpans along with the coffee in front of my nose and my distinguished gaze resting on them, so as to fetch me out of their heads one day, embalmed by this morning which smells of paling plane-tree leaves. And so we give life to each other . . . by existing, they on the far side of plate-glass windows and I over my coffee, like those pigeons on the church opposite, cooing instinctive breath into each other as if there were no such things as poisoned wheat and hawks.

To belong to the range of grays . . . That's why, incidentally, this birch tree keeps glinting through the work in progress. And those pigeons are being noted because they flatter grayness with the potential for muted rainbow hues to be seen in stained-glass windows.

Some man or other has seated himself on the terrace. He's keeping an eye open for the waiter, has noticed me and smoothed his hair (like mine!) with a fine hand. And my cup stained with coffee from my lip has caught my eye. I've smiled at it, and together we've allied ourselves against a wave of anonymity belched up by the cosmopolitan crowd.

Evening's arrived with refreshing darkness, all in linen bands and lace. Muffled in it, long drawn-out whistlings of police. Against that, the café's guts bloated with blazing light.

Paris, November 9, 197 . . .

Dear Sir,

Urgent professional matters have brought me, as you see, to Paris. I am staying in a city we both appreciate, although perhaps not for the same reason. It so happened that, on my way to a remarkably cheap and well-stocked bookshop, I went past the drugstore at Saint-Germain. I slowed down because I suddenly recalled that it was in fact one of the "ports" or "stations" on the map you had drawn.

I was struck by the relatively large number of young men, from sixteen to twenty years old, standing in entries or simply on the pavement. They were all, without exception, slender and quite good-looking. Dressed, indeed, with taste . . . (as you see, I am taking a snapshot of a cultural phenomenon for your use, avoiding any kind of judgment). The customers, on the other hand, seemed to me rather stocky, torso and little else. I was about to leave the place just then—because when all is said, it was a bazaar! if only someone had at least been crying his wares in a cheery patter, but all was silence—when a strange scene caught my attention. On the very edge of the pavement a boy is standing—oh, not more than eighteen years old—white turtle-

neck sweater under a lightweight dark jacket. Athlete's features.
All of a sudden another young man comes along, from la rue de
Rennes, but in a dustcoat as thin as tissue paper, unbuttoned so
that you can see a tanned chest and a medallion. And what do
you think—the one in the turtleneck took a step toward the
newcomer, and smiled. But the other one, toffee-nosed chap,
takes not the slightest notice of him. You are nothing but air. Go
grin at yourself in a mirror. And he walked past. And his thor-
oughbred, arrogant muzzle was saying: Ad maiora natus sum.

And then an unmajorly major came along as the next
minute, almost rubbing against the pavement, a Mercedes
(German!) drove up, out of which a round head leaned, so
shaven that it shone, and alongside it a small plump hand gra-
ciously extended an invitation to this same high-flying little
hairdresser with a faraway dream in his eyes. And what do you
think—the proud young esquire started to wiggle his little tail
and climbed in without hesitation!

And the other one—let us call him "of inferior rank"—
turned on his heel, looked around, and—just imagine it; later
I laughed myself sick at the whole thing—comes up to me with
the same significant smile as a moment before!

I fled the place, because sociology may be sociology, but one
cannot run the risk of ridicule after all . . . Afterward I remem-
bered your story about Olek . . . I checked over in my mind all
the individuals around the drugstore, but not one, really not one,
could compare to your friend, so full of the vitality of the folk.

You will smile when I add that the Paris air is full of leaves
now. Swarms of leaves, carried on a typical transverse wind,
lash passersby and those on the street corners . . . Quick, to a
café pot-bellied with light. In one of these, not far from that
fundamentally frivolous "bazaar," I am finishing off this letter,
adding many greetings from Paris . . .

Tarmstedt, December 4, 197 . . .
Kind Sir,
I write "kind" because "dear" means nothing these days! I

know what you mean when you scoff as you describe that evening at Saint-Germain, but it is because you were <u>standing aloof</u>. Please forgive this outspokenness in an old man, but you went about this in the same way as those relatives of mine who go off to Spain. They see battalions of priests uniformed in black there, and it seems to them that they have the right to sneer at God and immortality! Both the first case and the second are not so simple . . . And if you had gone with the one who winked so "significantly," maybe you would have forgotten, if only for one hour, your—please forgive an old man—foibles, you know: having to please everybody, not turn your backside to anybody, smile without remission, even if you have a terrible urge to shit!

You know, in Paris, in the old courtyards—I can see it from here!—the first frost will have just nipped geraniums at the windows. And from all sides there will be those smells of rot setting in . . . And that lad would have taken you through alleys and courtyards, up unlit staircases and along putrid little passages. And later maybe he would have begun to talk. And out from under that creature who was playing clever buggers on the street corner would have crawled a human being . . . no doubt lonely . . . like you . . . only less ingenious.

Precision is blinding you—how to put it?—precision at any price. Yes, yes, please believe me . . . And that is why you checked over the ones near the drugstore not as brothers in loneliness but as renegades from the ordinary world, to which you are proud to assign yourself.

Next time you suddenly realize that "the other sort" of people are all around you, you should flee from that spot as fast as possible! Because to fraternize means leaving your patent-leather shoes in the church porch and going barefoot, into the unknown . . . and that is not for you . . .

My dear man! Paris! A sin to walk around Paris like that, philosophizing and sneering, little and often! But I have <u>lived</u> there. And I grew there, luxuriantly, among those geraniums that flowered and rotted.

I shake your hand, a gingerbread pensioner,
like the Saint Nicholases that are filling shop windows here.
Thomas

"Fraternize"? I beg your pardon? For how much? One short hour or the night? Brotherhood at fixed rates. If you listened to such old blighters, apocrypha would take over from gospel. For him the sort of fellow who whores at the street corner—is a romantic dove with a money box at its arse. He does it in a garret with a view of the firmament.

Over there in the small town I've abandoned, dahlias will be lying and rotting to pale green. By now the women won't be cutting any more of them to put in the vinegar bottle that serves as penance for a vase in front of the little shrine all the May-long year.

"A sin to walk around Paris like that." It's different for him. He used to enjoy plunging into life, so he's dived to the depths, right down to the depths of his paid lover's pants to catch a glimpse of a well-known color!

The privy next to Wolański's joinery shop. Five, six, eight years old. Fifty years ago. In winter the plank's covered with golden hoarfrost so that sitting down, brrr! The answer's to squat. And squatting you see under you—the queen of autumn congealed to a proud pinnacle of ice. Since Martinmas journeymen and boys have been building this slender thing out of buckwheat gruel, maize, cabbage, and black bread thick with drippings and pork cracklings. And on the wallboards—hundreds of finger marks. Which finger? Whose? *Thomas's.* You want it, Tom asses it—his favourite color.

Now with her wing the jay's combing what was and what is, come what may, you only live once, jazz it up once! The beginning of the sentence is mine—but the end? The end, I suppose, is Thomas's.

Now the jay's perching on my head, a little coquette who's been tumbling in forget-me-nots and heather but with a beak daubed butcher fashion with the guts of a young tit. Let her comb that with her wing . . .

Did Thomas have a childhood? Go skating? Fishing? Up to the arse after crayfish? The beginning of the sentence is mine—but the end? The end comes from my mother's lips but incited by the insidious Thomas . . .

Childhood on a day like today. During the night the snows of all Slav fairy tales covered the world. By morning the old sun was all of a flutter in the sky, not knowing where to begin shooting rays or how many so as to flare like salt, like crystal, like a snowstorm of white bees in this air so that looking hurts. The first outing of an eight-year-old convalescent. On his thin little hands enormous mittens, where every now and again our Mam has to play Hunt the Thimble for his tiny fingers. And such trimness in this Sunday kitchen garden, such silence, that all at once our Mam hits the trunk of a plum tree with a merry hand and—cages of cabbage whites, packets of postage stamps, powder compacts fly open! With the connivance of that old sun, snorting with laughter. And the little boy, the lad, is off at full tilt, shaking the snowy crowns of the trees, across the kitchen garden, across the world, taking heart forever . . .

We correspond, pretending that it's "an exchange of views," but I can see he's trying to convert me. In his last letter he was making fun of my "shitting trauma." He maintains that it's women teachers and priests who've instilled in us Poles that mania for washing our hands and a superstitious fear of breasts at the backs of our bodies, from between which oozes the unending serpent of our uncleanliness, expelled from paradise.

After New Year. He seemed such a tough customer—and now he's hobbling and in a bad way because the poor old chap's heart is giving out. He makes out he's taking it cheerfully.

. . . so that, for the time being, I am not allowed to ride a bike, stand on my hands, or throw cupboards through windows, but, my dear man, what is worse is that here in my head everything is going to pieces, too. You know . . . by this stage thoughts are not thoughts anymore, they are washed out and laundered with bleach for an old beggar's ragbag . . . You already know Olek, Yazit. No, you do not know Yazit yet, but when we meet sometime, I will tell you about him as well. Yesterday, before I dropped off, I tried to call to mind a number of odds and ends Olek and I got up to . . . Nothing doing. Just as if you, sir, had clipped Olek's silhouette out of a towel in a station urinal and told him to stand up . . . You remember his breeches. Nothing. Just a hint of his eyes has been preserved, but even they are paler than the ones I described to you . . . So I am searching my brain like mad for Paris! If only it were possible to run as far as those chestnut trees at Saint-Germain . . . my dear man . . . whatever I manage to glimpse in this dozy state is trash. The canvas of a mere dauber, the color laid on atrociously . . . Even the wine in its little carafe is anemic as medicine.

And so, not to lose the dregs of faith and hope, I unbutton my fly and pull out my cockerel. Outside the window, no leaves, not a bird, only soot from nearby factories settling on the pane. Not even snow this New Year afternoon. And so we sit, the pair of us. By this time, soot is indistinguishable from gloom. And I see that it is time to set about writing this letter . . .

Ostend, January 15, 197 . . .
Dear Thomas,
He has never been <u>there</u> before, you will exclaim on seeing the place where this was posted. To tell the truth, I am a frequent visitor to this somewhat stolid "pearl of the seas" with fries in her curls. I am staying at Touring, a minuscule hotel, where I am rereading your letter, as full of goodwill as ever, but this time more grizzled with loneliness, as it were.

I know what your growing frustration means only too well,

but that is the way it is with memories by this stage. One time we look for homegrown strawberries and pale grubs crawl out; on another occasion, we are daydreaming beside the portrait of a girl with a posy of white carnations when a troop of sweaty recruits cannons into the photograph, farting starkers.

I should very much like to pay you a visit but at present have to pore over my students' labors. Over here, January is all the more burdensome for teaching purposes as it follows the winter vacation's incitements to idleness . . .

Here, in an Ostend grown gray as a spider's web, where wind dries out the sands and packs them with some species of bird that flies along the coastline, no doubt heading south, I keep wondering whether you might not have a go at <u>painting</u> Paris for yourself. I know, as I have seen a pencil in your fingers, that you are capable of compelling the return of streets and houses, stairways, doors and little pots of flowers, and the <u>life</u> that linked those places and objects with a voice, with voices and the revved-up blood of youth.

Heaven, once painted, cannot disintegrate.

Thighs, once flesh-tinted, cannot run to fat.

Yazit's eyes will be tender and playful forever, and Olek's breeches will stick out like a woodpecker from a pine tree! And I guarantee that you yourself will flush red in the light of those paints or crayons given point and texture in the narrow alleyways of Paris!

I squeeze your hand heartily (inasmuch as it is not preoccupied . . .)

A treatise could be written on the creaking of cart wheels. But what's the use—today it's already too late, as the last wheels turn into coffee tables deluxe under glass, and on top of the glass, the pipe and whiskey of a director in slippers warmed by the television set.

And by this time one carter I know has fitted car wheels. And that cart of his rolls smooth as satin over the asphalt, off with the cabbage to market . . .

Aah! Acacia wheels! In my day every stork and its mate knew that the best ones are acacia. Because woodworm doesn't get at them. And it used to build its nest on them. But today? Neither cart wheels nor storks today. Only woodworm.

The creaking wheel that keeps going is obviously Thomas. Besides, he's stopped creaking by this time. The spirit's come back to him. He's taking longer and longer walks and is painting.

. . . when I started, what came to me first were the streets where I used to hang out with the boys, before going up to one of our rooms. Now I am painting them in person, my special ones that I loved, you know, in Paris, Warsaw, and Marseilles . . .

For some reason I suddenly looked out of the window a few days ago, just like that . . . with the kind of look that wants to see, and I saw a jay. And in her wake—my dear man!—such a springtime suddenly burgeoned in me that there was too little space for it between earth and heaven! Such a spring with rains, bright rays, that I hurled myself into the painting of my excursion to Lwów with such an adorable boy . . . but I have not told you about that yet.

Today the chalks are on the table again. And on the drawing pad—my lads! We racket about there with complete abandon. If it doesn't want to go in—then Vaseline! Wherever it floods, it's the goods! Not so?

My dear man! My memory is flowing back so liberally that the numbers of those houses write themselves down with my chalk, and even the lampposts—as if I were copying them from a photograph! . . . I see the flaking plaster in the little hotel room . . . that I used to look at, when I did it with Yazit, then he with me . . . And the beds! My dear man . . . In the evenings, when night was just beginning to creep out of chimneys, those beds of ours would creak so that fluttering bats were scared of us! Because windows were open. And the sawmill gets going between us!

Whoever took it into his head at that time to dose himself regularly, philosophize, have little cups of café crème, and hide

Paris behind a newspaper? . . . Life was for living . . . the bitch!

Well, and a polite little formula as usual . . . So have at my pen:

Brussels, May 14, 197 . . .
My dear sir,
Keep it up! I have read your letter aloud—like a proclamation! Little was lacking, and I all but started to regret that I had not been there . . . you summoned up those times so jauntily, with all the dash of a genuine madcap student. I am glad that you are having a go at illustrating your experiences, all the more so as you really do have something to illustrate!

I have no end of work at this time of year. What's more, in the evenings after supper and while listening to the news on the radio, I read and write letters to our Mam in Poland and, as you see, to friends. I listen to music as well (Mozart, but only for the violin). In the mornings, I read the paper with my coffee for a change. I have a shot at viewing the world over the top of it, so as to see farther than my nose or navel . . .

All the best for more drawings and a champagne boost for yourself . . .

There were storms in June. There was a feeling of something strange happening to the air. As if up there a newly appointed meteorologist had set about putting things to rights. People labeled the sky with whatever sayings and old wives' tales they possessed. June passed them by, unruly and rampant, lashing them with thunderbolts.

Meadows and gardens were sweating. Elders and lime trees were steeped in nectar. Bees trailed a pale tress of wax toward drowsy surfeit.

Was it really like that? Or at the same time did the author want, that's to say, did he feel the need to envisage his own midsummer in just that way? And transcribe his enchantment in such a glowing little landscape? That's it, as if he needed some transient subject matter to bear off Thomas's affairs, so as to keep them at a distance on some uncharted sandbank. Then he, the author back here, will grow conscious of this hiatus. He'll put his hand to his brow and what he'll envisage—as far as the eye can see—will be a valley.

Along it, along this valley of snowball trees, already moving toward this work in progress written here at this moment in time, is a tiny traveler. It amuses us to watch how, little by little, he keeps growing amidst the kind of gestures by which it's so easy for us to recognize travelers born to animate valleys. This is heartening, this pretense of ours that we don't know who's coming and that, since this is so, we must exercise due caution . . .

Ooooh!—now we recognize him. It's the German Thomas, the man who ought not to be right. He's brandishing enormous paws with nails hacked by a hatchet and he's saying something. As if he knows that we're leaning over a balcony suspended in a June storm and are lending a benevolent ear. Ah! now he's shouting:

Benefactor sir,
I really do not know how to thank you for your excellent advice and for the fact that you have been willing to stoop as far as my gutter fate . . .

You were expecting that sort of tone, OK? Instead of which, ungrateful Thomas simply shared his pleasure with you. He was sure there was no need to spell out for you the role your friendly letter played, not to mention the advice that I should paint . . . Once again, dear sir, that culture . . . that you-must-you-should-you-ought-not-say-how-do-you-do-stand-up-straight-aaaah-have-you-said-thank-you?-Whaat?-Say-thank-you-im-med-i-ate-ly-About time too!

And the mother cuffs her offspring on the muzzle because she is on edge, and he has been wool-gathering and did not say thank you in time.

I have never been gushing as far as feelings go. I put up with greetings and farewells like a dentist's efforts. When other people waggle their hands and "send kisses," I—how to put it?—deplore that everything is so brittle here, shake my head resignedly over myself, over us—that's all. I had a good laugh because you write so terribly seriously about your morning paper. My dear man . . . that culture of yours, so as to be in a position, right after waking, to make a precise count of corpses from the night just slept through, to swallow—along with your coffee—gangsters, ministers, an earthquake, and a new record for standing on one's head . . . I ask myself—though you will never be able to answer this—what this has to do with you, with me, with our life?

You know, I had the chance of listening for hours to the tales of a Japanese who was studying in Paris but <u>who</u> <u>lived</u> <u>with</u> <u>us</u>, and when we had a fantastic gang mill, four or six of us together, Yazit would run for a kilo of ham, long loaves, and wine . . . and we would tell each other about our lives at the four corners of the world. My dear man, what stories those were! The brother of this Japanese used to fish for pearls. He had a place of his own. And so no one could spy on him, he and his girl would go there, pretending to be a couple in love . . . One time this brother comes back to the shallows and laughs at his girlfriend. She says: You've got something? Big? And she can see by his expression that it is something out of the ordinary . . . Show! she shouts. And he smiles from ear to ear as only a happy Japanese can and answers: For you . . . an engagement one. Look for yourself, but no hands! Having said this, he drops on all fours, like a seal emerging from the depths . . . And the naughty bitch found it!

I enclose two little pictures. Everything taken from nature. Only you will not recognise from their pricks who is cultured and who is an oaf, who came in his own Mercedes and who gives handouts in public urinals . . .

I greet you, my dear sir, affectionately,
Thomas

Dear Thomas,
Thank you—oh, please forgive this bourgeois habit—for

your letter and daubs. For my part, I value your outspokenness, which is not to say that what you write does not rouse me to object. Not everything, however. For instance, I agree with you that the gutter press and its sex scandals have nothing to do with culture, or our lives for that matter. But suppose I really am looking for real life in a serious paper, trying to distinguish the light and dark currents that stream through our great European river? Suppose I am looking for facts there which might help to sustain my faith in man, man perceived with less ardent eyes than those of your Japanese . . . Suppose I am intrigued by riddles above the waist, the dignity of men who are beaten, kicked, hungry, and saved thanks to evangelical or political cranks . . .

The more I get absorbed in conversation with you (and now I am looking at these charming little pictures), the more often the word egoists *comes to mind.*

Right at the bottom, on this little picture, you have put a date . . . By that time I was going to grammar school. My throat constricted, I was reading in Forward *the names of Spanish towns, bombarded, defended, stormed and bombarded afresh and . . . taken by Fascist tanks. My dear man! Guernica was crumbling in ruins . . . anyone who believed . . . in man was walking through mountains and forests, at night, like a robber! Across the Pyrenees so as to enlist under the standard of the International Brigades . . .*

That was my first war. Newspapers wrote about it. At that time only children had the right to illiteracy.

Please forgive this exchange of frankness for frankness . . .

I send cordial greetings.

Well—a dialogue at last. Not chats with smiling innuendos but a dialogue. Is it possible—not even a matter by now of whether one has the right, but is it possible . . . simply to cut free from history in the making . . . Paris under the Occupation. The first concert or art exhibition organized by the Germans—*those* at the preview! Painters, dancers, critics

. . . And what's more, describing arcs with eyes, apolitical eyelashes, and pacifist buttocks . . . greasers. But don't let Thomas think it's as a Pole that I'm attacking him. I simply can't accept their intellectual nonpresence, their lack of solidarity in dark moments of national history. Some reach for weapons . . . while *they*—bull on bull, as if the-birds-do-sing-hey-ding-a-ding-ding . . . strong in their philosophy of "If you can keep it flowing / The going's bound to be good."

Today I no longer know if apples were falling helpless into grass of their own accord, pecked by capricious starlings, whether sugar beets were falling into the mud from top-heavy carts, when I started reading Thomas's next letter.

You were—please forgive me—just a kid who wanted to perform some exploit. And I suppose those barricades were a party treat for youngsters in poor countries . . . where "heroism" comes easier than a pair of boots. There, old fellows pushing fifty get the booze and the whores while kids' heads are stuffed with all and sundry who wear fetters like adornments . . . and cut cannon to pieces with scythes . . . My dear man! In Europe at that time, how many shouted "no pasaran"? *Maybe a few hundred . . . well, maybe a few thousand. And the rest? The rest lived* <u>for</u> <u>themselves</u>. *Please listen—because they had the right to live! And we in Paris had the right to live our lives without the seal of history on our naked, private arses! And what happened yesterday in Vietnam? The Pentagon installed hell in the house of the Lord God and from that vantage point rained down fire, sulfur, and Gomorrah on the Vietnamese . . . And young Americans, those most ardent of pacifists, what were they to do? What* <u>could</u> *they do?! Get together at Woodstock. You remember that ants' nest of boys and girls, those hills submerged in rock and shrieking and singing. They did not even notice whether it was day or night. They shrieked their protest* <u>through</u> <u>life</u>.

My dear man—what is a body guilty of that first these, then those order it to impale itself on bayonets? Get them off my happiness! An old man is saying this to you, one who knows the meaning of a lifelong day sustained until twilight . . .

Dear friend, <u>our lot</u> found themselves in this situation anyway . . . alongside the others from the barricades. You know very well that the Hitlerites packed homosexuals off to concentration camps. But nothing is said about this today . . . I will tell you something else. If I had a son and the sort of swinishness you and I lived through was going to start up, don't you worry, I would indeed advise him then . . .

I'm reading, reading this letter, and thoughts lash about in my head like a flayed eel. And this eel falls into snow. And through this snow, these snows—soldiers. Rifles on mere strings. But they know these strings will make nooses to string up Fascists!

> Past pine wood and forest
> through places burned to ashes
> by bombs marked with crosses
> And snow falls on them as they go
> And they snatch their heads back not to crash down
> so that
> I shall grow bloodier than snow . . .

A mailbox where we gather masses of mushrooms smelling of discreet night, gather flowers and worlds franked with a juicy berry. The opening of the casket . . . THERE IT IS! A large gray envelope standing on end. Instead of flopping down to the bottom it's poised for fingers. Thick, with a Pole's address written by a pen steeped in a gothic inkwell. A dozen pictures. And not a word.

A square in Marseilles. Open windows. Light of a summer morning's being poured onto the pavement where all that remains of night is a banana skin and a leaky condom. And in the middle of the square a confused youngster, because in his place I'd no more know whether to go with this rascal on the left or this cutthroat on the right; because both are so bursting with youth that it's plain to see. And from a window, watching this muscular bartering, gazing at this display of supple wares, a *female* with flying buttresses. And over there at the end of the street, ladies and gentlemen, through an open window you may observe . . . the sequel to the bargain struck here: two naked men standing eye to eye and chest to chest.

Let's look for our acquaintance. No—he's not here. Instead this is a little genre picture to which the all-but-sociological title bears witness, if nothing else: "11:00 A.M. and business in progress already."

O-oh—here's Thomas. This is clearly a small hotel for short lets! Please observe. In this miserable little room with walls that permit red brick to shine through, on a mattress with emerald stripes, lies a dark man, strikingly handsome. He's resting on his stomach wearing just a singlet with red and white stripes. Arms and white untanned buttocks tattooed with hearts and anchors. And over him kneels a naked fair-haired man with a gold watch on his wrist, kneeling between the other's dirty feet and at him. And looking on at this ecstasy's some gangster type, also in a red singlet with white stripes. His hair's black, luxuriant and gleaming with brilliantine, black eyebrows, too. On each bicep a girl of reasonably easy virtue depicted merely legs astraddle. On each thigh the gangster's got a design of the female pudenda, simplified to a triangle with eyelashes round it and a mouth in the middle. He's raising his right hand in an engaging rakish gesture. A luxury cigarette's burning itself out in this hand, but with his left hand he's expressing his personality roused to the utmost limit of passion. Which seems to call the bluff of the fellow's rather photogenic smile. And the floor offers a précis of its contents: butts scattered here while over there's a rosy condom freshly used, and in addition a porcelain chamber pot, half full of blond urine . . .

The pictures are endlessly pushed aside, rearranged, and selected. This is Thomas's country. I walk through it in silence over and over again and suddenly—lean over the iron bedstead where "they" are. And draw this island's odors in through my nose . . . And the seconds grow more and more sluggish . . . and through the window floats the green bottle with fat Anielka in it. She disembarks, pushes both lads off the emerald mattress, and lays her white self on her back, her violet hell's mouth uppermost! And by now there's no one but her in this room except for some woman's profile in a holy picture. Who pretends there's nothing worth viewing and she's merely holding her hands together, up to the stars for good measure. But in point of fact viewing's going on. And for me in this little mitten, it's so warm, so cosy, fat Anielka smiles like a, like a, like a . . .

Must escape these impudent bodies. Must cover this up. Must clamp down this kicking game with another landscape of the Thomist island. If only with this alley. Slap it down! Clamped down and covered up now by this rubbish dump with its champagne bottles and asparagus tins once deluxe, right next to bedsprings that used to rock bodies but today lie here, slept to death.

Dear Thomas,

I am writing belatedly to thank you for your invitation to an exhibition of, I suspect, unique painting, with doors open to only one spectator. I appreciate your trust. I have traveled through your world, along the August paths through heathery places, passing bodies agape from parching heat. I do not have such "fiery" memories. First love—better if we do not speak about it. Instead, have you no plans for some small trip to one of your neighboring countries? I know a certain kingdom where you would be cordially received.

A strange thought has suddenly struck me . . . whether, if circumstances had worked out differently, I would have ended up like you?

I shake your hand . . .

Thomas couldn't come. Each time in the very near future. Maybe in winter. Maybe by spring. He doesn't invite me to his place as he's got distant relatives round his neck, difficult, what's more, to explain by letter . . .

First love . . . we recognize it, we recognize . . . when it is over. But before it comes—it is so plastered with platitudes like posters on a Paris kiosk . . . that you are left groping around and the place echoes with Heine or some other anguished Francophile philosopher on a meatless and spiritless diet. Yes, yes . . . which of us has not breathed a lost name, giving the coup de grâce to a third-class provincial whore or a fist surprised by the sudden passion of its master?

It crossed my mind . . . suppose you tried to describe that "first love" of yours? If for no other reason, to see how much of it is left . . . To set your cupboard to rights for Easter. Since maybe there are only one-eyed, crippled moths in this cupboard by now?

I am glad that you have been trying to grasp what <u>our</u> life is like, our love, what the <u>body</u> is like!—the body that you have feared since childhood. You are still young, I tell you, nothing is certain, maybe you will still meet some woman who will help you to save yourself . . . Because only in pairs is it possible to press on through this world that's besmirched from earth right up to heaven . . . For someone on his own it is the same as with meals—one does not want to set the table and eats slices of sausage straight out of the wrapping. In any case, you know what that is like . . .

And one more thought for today: You are not and never will be one of <u>us</u>. Only your sort of people can make a mistake about you. To your sort it may seem that those poppy scarves of yours and those ties embroidered with peacock's eyes . . . that all this signifies something. But all it means is you like, even idolize, yourself. I shall be frank. You are too careful, too concerned for the future, to break out into such a life as mine, to—as you put it so charmingly—"end up" like me. Of course, it intrigues you . . . perhaps even tempts you, but at the very idea of sticky bodies standing exposed—you want to run for soap and towel in no time. Uncleanness fascinates your temperament, but you view it through a bourgeois windowpane as a cat views dogs wallowing in gutters that secrete pus from the car plague. You are afraid of risk and maybe that is why you are virtuous?

But _us_! Enough for the nose to flare that trail in the station air, you know, the trail that each of us can latch onto blindfolded . . . And next moment I have got an eye full of the hot stare of those already waiting there. My dear man, what splendid shamelessness! By now, arms are elbowing each other as they cross each other's path, and that strange carp is stirring in my hand while mine is not alone. Let us go away. Anywhere, provided there are four walls of greenery or night, the screw gets going, no matter how many shames we render shameless! My dear man . . . none of us makes an ass of himself with phrases like Though-I-love-you-madly-you've-gone-to-sleep-So-I'll-shit-for-you-then-you'll-eat-you-creep . . . No listening to idle talk, but bodies at work. Then he gets up and I get up and it pours off us! And we have seedy muzzles. And with these slimy snouts we look at each other and laugh. And with one of those selfsame muzzles I am looking at you at this moment, so that you may perceive _who_ _you_ _are_ _not_.

I send you affectionate greetings,
Yours, Thomas

Dear Thomas,

A real man ought not dabble in secretions. You get my meaning. But you would like me to lay hands on these once-rosy guts that I have been in the habit of force-feeding with violets, mignonette, and breast-beating, and to squeeze them. Do not let us amuse ourselves with this kind of experiment . . . after all, we know what will come out the other end. So instead of the memoirs of today's man, I am sending you notes that are some-

1958. A holiday summer, summer with the old sun repeatedly torn off the calendar by an indolent hand, full of reflections, of open-mouthed amazements at . . . if only at those huge and shaggy leaves from under which the traditional arses of Polish pumpkins emerge, pretending to be beach bums but in fact recalling concentration camp latrines.

A summer of paths beaten hard between rows of wheat by running barefoot kids who'd been prying . . . "There, mister, there under the sour old pear tree, Mr. Józek Kruniu at the lady . . . " And I stand on tiptoe and see how vigorously he's planing the councillor's softly whimpering widow . . .

And then this central European air annexed by feathered and hymenopterous creatures, full of green steel magpies busy disemboweling other birds' chicks, air split by the giddy flight of a dragonfly simulating interest in a Lilliputian landscape of three-storied crowfoot.

All this covered by a twelve-inch layer of slushy snow which we're wading through as if on stilts in 1938 . . . still in winter overcoats but already unbuttoned with an eye to "casting a clout." And she peeps over her shoulder, over her pigtail, snorts with hoity-toity merriment and leaves me in this thaw, shoes soaking . . . while she runs to the villa and with a cup of boiling hot chocolate in her hand looks at me through the curtain as, hidden behind a telegraph pole, I proceed to catch cold gazing at her window. And she calls her six sisters and even the curtain feels foolish about having to veil so much staring and giggling, hands over mouths.

To be sitting in a holiday armchair ("If it's too hard for you, just you say, I'll fetch you a cushion, in a bit I'll bring you some wild strawberries and cream, I'm just washing them"), our Mam hanging over me. She'd foreseen it all: "Poor kid, that girl will have her bit of fun and make you pay for it, then throw you away like a rag."

"In the afternoon we'll drop over to a place near Mrzygłód—Pluta, you know, that postman's got hives over there in the forest, wild honey like resin, not sweet, it really scalds your mouth like rotgut," my brother hanging over me.

My eyelids are warm and rest cosily on my eyes so that the twilight's ruby under them. Suddenly a noise of dragging feet and a ringing of horseshoes on stone make themselves heard in this twilight. And now a pony emerges from the leaves of a crumbling, moldering calendar. And on this pony First Love. With the bandiness of her forty-year-old thighs she squeezes the poor beast, which goes through the motions of neighing eagerly, but it's a rasping cough that spews from its throat. She's no doubt mounted it for a joke, no doubt they've said to her: "He's arrived. He'll be bound to want to write about you, so do something youthful— well, girlish—let those braids fly loose, you know, like this in the breeze, look, the mountains are cornflower blue just in time, you won't find a better background. Purse your knees."

And the poor cow believed them. And giddyap to recapture her old role. And she doesn't even see the vermin scattering from off the pony, and she parades herself on this stiffening carrion along the path where there's the

> forlorn dome of a church with nightbirds, owls
> timbered ruins left by the belfry to rot
> past the belfry fruit run wild in brambles
> and in those brambles tombs lest we forget.

But this is nothing to her; she just rides along the valley for her own sake, quivering with fat all the way. And the pony falls into a time the color of squashed moths on a mirror because this woman's buttocks weigh like a smuggler's great packs.

Clippety-clop to the parish church! And she hurriedly

dons her grammar school uniform in the porch, and, seams splitting, parades like this up the middle of the nave where the little hand of Our Lady's divided the people according to custom, Holeynesses on the right and Flapdanglers on the left. But even so all eyes look up under the vaulting. Because there in wings and swords, juggling with halos in their spare time, the papal police force has its barracks. See, at this moment they're looking at me because they've sniffed out an unclean thought in my noddle. Because I'm looking at a female martyr who's exhibiting to the church public the tongs, still smoking, with which executioners kept trying to unscrew her nipples so as to drink their fill of virgin's milk straight from the bottle. So I run away to a male martyr, but he's so tastefully stuck with arrows that the Lord God Himself's had to give up trying to stroke him.

But our Mam sees my agitation and looks at me with compassion.

And First Love journeys on through fumes of incense, and by now you can't even smell out the pony that was giving off an odor of sour broth made from forty-year-old bones. And all you can hear is middle-aged women clicking rosaries of their own teeth through their fingers, and all you can hear is young girls boxing themselves under the breast with their little fists to scare that bat in their knickers that never stops yawning with its entire tiny raspberry throat. And then with all speed, a throwing of lily-white litanies by the armful, of cruciform white nights on the marble church floor so as to kill that drooling flittermouse, to crucify it on the shed with nails so it wouldn't ever again set an abdominable ambush for boys.

And so as to put a hole through this picture—I stretch out my hand. It meets a closed door. Then in the opposite direction till my fingers break into houses with windows torn out, beyond which is unbreached night howling in a kicked and beaten voice. From these windows, boys, a livid procession, all got up as if for the Resurrection, though this one's legless, this one's holed in the forehead, and they dress ranks. And innocent infants appear in a throng, neat, it's true, but little heads seemingly slightly crumpled against the edge of a wall, and from their diminutive baskets they scatter an Occupation winter that is clean, that is nice and white. And those young lads, as if on command, abruptly start to piss! And they write with precision as if for a school book, on this winter without spring:

I shall grow bloodier than life . . .

Please, dear Thomas, forgive these slides that have begun to stink of corpses, like the nails of a rag-and-bone man digging in putrescent trash cans. But I bequeath them to you without any touching up. Since that year, since 1958, I wash my hands regularly and clean my nails, so not one of those evil violets smelling of earwax wiggles in front of my nose. But when I happen to go past those windows over there, you know, where it is all

fruit run wild in brambles
and in those brambles tombs . . .

then I squeeze my stomach with my diaphragm—so that my body retches with a foul, unfocused voice! Or I let fly some word, to the wind as it were, but my word knows that it must—yoicks! attack this house and this place with a filth as corrosive as acid. My dear sir, each time I am there, I circle that house, uttering various conjurations-maledictions, so that all that has happened there is preserved for the future, mummified, conserved by my venom, so that even if there is some office in that house now, the she-clerks' eyes are darkened because of my execrations. Without me—that time back there would have fallen to pieces. Who would have remembered that pony? But, Thomas, I can wake those years up. Like a kapellmeister, I know how to rouse into noise and lamentation: When the forest used to be We were nowhere at all The forest will continue still

When we're nowhere at all . . . Even poor Mam sighs when she sees that I am laying out these corpses in their little coffins, lined up neatly like a row of black beehives. And with a motherly hand she tries to drive off, scatter this lugubrious beastliness that makes music without ceasing. But Thomas, I promised . . . on my honor, you understand . . . that I would never forget . . . Today . . . today I would have walled these memories in with bottles of champagne, so that they would sweat themselves to death in these underground cells and even catch cold like me that time under the telegraph pole.

Last summer, I got myself up as smartly as possible, a tie that . . . well, imagine it for yourself . . . and shoes and a silk shirt . . . and by chance I go slowly past that prewar villa over there . . . And what do you think—I fell in with their old servant, who—as she told me—was also going that way purely by chance. I kissed her, though she was a simple country girl. I gave her a few dollars so that she could buy some little thing for herself. And that certainly got around, because since then, whenever I go that way by chance, everyone greets me very politely. And they congratulate the mother of such a son. Eeeeh . . . let us forget it.

You compared me to a cat . . . it is true, I come back here like a cat that is trying to find warm, dry paths again. I prefer this to doglike scatter-barked happiness, to that doglike shamelessness, to—please forgive me—that doglike cocky boorishness. When I was young, I was taught . . . and I try not to forget it, that not only Sir Prick inhabits my body but above all Sir Reason.

I bring this epistle to an end, brought out into the light partly thanks to you, and turn toward you a freshly shaved face rubbed with eau de cologne and along with it a friendly glance from its eyes.

Yours . . .

To get good tea, first you have to warm the pot with boiling water, then put in the tea leaves and pour boiling water over them. Let it stand for five minutes . . .

When it's snowing like today, Wednesday, at precisely four in the afternoon, Earl Grey in a glass is liquid sun almost like a fox-fur muff glowing ruddy on the road to church on a winter morning round the hands of Maryśka, who has a tongue of raspberry jam except that it's more rasping. Such a time, marked by gulps of such tea, is part of the pleasure I suppose a squirrel knows in the depths of its winter sleep, heaped over with dreams.

And the telephone snatched just such a creature, looking at November through double-glazed windows, from his meditation. Thomas! He suggests there's a chance of meeting, as at midday on Saturday somebody over there, a neighbor or whatever, has a business appointment in Astenet just across the Belgian border. And that if I could get as far as that we could spend the whole afternoon together . . . The other fellow won't have finished his business till 7:00 P.M. . . . So we'll meet just before lunch in the restaurant of the Château Thor hotel.

The train glides as if through fog because there's a powder of fine aluminium snow falling. From the station at Eupen—by bus right up to the hotel itself. The air's brisk here, almost mountain air. Thomas is standing with his nose close to the windowpane. I spot him and he's caught sight of me. In no time we're in the hall. We're standing on a creaky oak floor almost in dusk. Only hunting horns of some kind to sun us from the walls. Perhaps better that it's twilight, come to that—eyes can't see eyes and we can transmit emotion through our hands. We shake them time and again.

In mine host's footsteps to the dining room. Walls covered with frescoes above a hearth to end all hearths where you could burn whole pollard willows: dated 1600. And on the ceiling an enormous bunch of grapes in high relief.

Haunch of venison as forests are close by. A half-bottle of Burgundy since the beast is noble. And this castle, too, which, despite the hearth, has turned out to be the surviving . . . wing of a farmhouse.

If you were to go up to the loft and move aside those grapes big as bull's balls stuck like swallows' nests to the ceiling, it would be possible to glimpse the heads of two men, one bald and the other balding within a garland of little angels' feathers. And lower down, their hands on a white tablecloth, not far from a wine stain lavishly sprinkled with salt. Thomas's fingers are teasing some crumb while the Pole's hands clip and trim the air. Now they're in suspended motion and seem to want to stop Thomas from speaking. But Thomas retreats with his rollicking laugh into the recesses of his chair.

In the depths, behind his small eyes, windows with tiny panes of new-formed ice and beyond them a world of stripped orchards, of forests where jays are already reading out the names of hares that will face the firing squad at the Christmas Eve shoot.

When the owner's son, willowy Emil, brought two coffees, Thomas took a tiny pillbox out of his waistcoat, swallowed something out of it, and drank a sip.

"You know, that time when my heart almost conked out—that was the second time around . . . these pills as a result . . . "

And he smiled. And reached into his breast. From under . . . his shirt he took out an envelope just like the one in which he sent me his French daubs. He smoothed it out on the tablecloth.

" . . . why don't you keep it at your place. It'll be better that way. Why should anyone find it when I croak someday . . . But at your place . . . " (he smiles) " . . . these little pictures will stay put as if they were at mine . . . "

And he lays his hand on mine. And squeezes it affectionately, withdrawing his own at once. But he's shaking his head thoughtfully again like that time behind the coach window on the gilded Grand'Place in Brussels.

" . . . I've invited you here to tell you . . . because writing isn't the same . . . about Yazit."

"The tattoo? Those eyes?"

"Yes. Those eyes, that boy, that love. Listen . . . It was the same sort of November or December, I don't know which by this time, as today. I never used to wear gloves, but that evening I had to bury my hands in my pockets, there was such a hurricane of dry snow.

"I'm walking on my own through Montparnasse, and I see in front of me some lad or other wants to cross over, but he's waiting for the cars to go past. I pass him—and he looked round. And we both smiled. He was wearing a beret. He quickened his pace. As if in a hurry. But I had time, you know, to see under that Basque beret was a very beautiful face. You know, a thoroughbred type, swarthy. I notice straightaway that he isn't French but from somewhere in Africa. Well, OK. We walk a short distance like that, and it's obvious he's slim-waisted as his sweater fits tight. He goes into a pissoir. Aha. Then me too. Nobody, just us. He's standing next to me—and you know, the world over, it starts the same way. And he says:

"'Shall we go?'

"'Of course,' I say.

"And now slanting across the street, just blinking our eyes because of the snow. The hotel's nearby. I don't know if you're familiar with that part . . . near the Duguesclin restaurant . . . The proprietress must have known him, as she gave him a key without a word.

"My dear man—we'd hardly got inside—and he's stripping already. He just keeps a short pullover on, navy blue with a rolled collar . . . but lower down—Lord—a whipple-tree fit to put a wedding to flight! A swarthy lizard, but he has these cornflower eyes and laughs, because he sees I can't take my eyes off him any more than off a work of art. It's obvious he has no time to spare, because he makes a grab at me—and on to the bed. You know, we're both ruttish, because I'm straight up, too. We go berserk, while our fingers get demanding and tough. But all the time he's in this little pullover. So I run my hand along his thigh—and hey presto! up with the sweater. And he breaks loose! Raving. But I had time to catch sight of a green tattoo inscribed in thick Arabic script.

"'What's up? What are you hiding?' I say, because I was surprised by this pullover in bed and this terror when I touched it. 'But it's beautiful,' I say, 'those letters on your belly . . . '

"And he's kneeling beside me and covering my mouth with his hand:

"'Stupid,' he says, 'if you knew what it means, you wouldn't pay me . . . and what's more you'd kick me downstairs like a dog!'

"I stood up. Without a word, I took I don't remember how much out of my wallet, but certainly twice as much as he was expecting, and say:

"'Here you are. If you like, you can go. I'll pay for the hotel . . . You don't need to do anything else or tell . . . Since you haven't told anyone up to now what you've got written there.'

"But you know—while I was smoking, quietly smoking—he sat down Turkish-style, looked at me, and says:

"'Do you really want to look at it?'

"'Why yes,' I say, and see that somehow, you know, he's touched . . .

"'Well then, look!' And he lifted up his pullover. Under his navel, in the middle of his olive belly, ran a blue-green inscription, tangled and weird.

"Believe me . . . if he were to stand like that here, in front of us, now . . . the same sort of rapture would take hold of you as did me there, in the Paris hotel . . . I started to kiss him feverishly on that African writing, incomprehensible to me . . . but he looked at me wretchedly . . . put his hand on my cheek . . . and drew his pullover down at once. And it grew rather quiet. After a while, he looks at me and suddenly pulls himself up straight and starts like this:

"'I'll tell you what this inscription means . . . but . . . you won't be disgusted by me afterward?'

"My dear man—how can't I start kissing him all over his body, hugging him . . . "

And as he says this, his head suddenly grows larger. Look!—it must be three feet across already. And mine's probably no smaller! And our eyes have grown to match. Thomas's are like woodpecker holes encircling sky. And through them you can see an African world with its horizon and mirage full of promises. Now a sheikh on a magnificent charger soars over the dunes, now a caravan and a hundred Arabs driving camels with bloody whips so as to deliver alive to their destination slaves hidden in first-class tea . . . And close by, a fat Arab's yawning. Now he's gorging himself with something . . . must be a leg of lamb done with plums . . . Now he's choosing a dessert from a brass tray with his gross fingers. Turkish delight. Turkish delight. Turkish delight. He's stuffed these morsels in his mouth. But here's twelve-year-old Yazit in front of him. And he's on his knees. So the Arab pushes one Turkish delight out of his mouth into the youngster's with his tongue. But Yazit does nothing, just swallows and swallows. And he's plump. And succulent.

And through the other eye you can see how this man of property's taken Yazit up in front of him, making love to him appallingly again and again.

And through Thomas's huge ear you can hear night in Tangiers, hear the groaning of twelve-year-old Yazit as sailors give him the coup de grâce, down to the deck . . .

And suddenly this Yazit's laid himself down here in front of us on the dining table in the Château Thor, pierced to the last gasp by those sailors of forty years ago. I pretend that I'm not stunned, that I'm not overwhelmed by disgust. I can keep up appearances as no one's monitoring my blood under the table, noting how it rouses like a cock in a cage. And Yazit doesn't even open his eyes, he's been so battered.

What's this? A rabble of Arabs with the fat one at its head

bursts into the hotel dining room! Full speed ahead!—to flog sick little Yazit with whips, to scrawl glossy black stripes across his back, bright crimson stripes! Thomas darts a glance at me and hisses:

"Look now!"

And they turn him on his back and stand on his arms and legs. And they laugh, the sort of laugh that comes from a stiff prick. And they sit, arse bare, on Yazit's sobbing face.

"Look, look!—now comes the last word in swinishness!"

Some Arab or other with a hawkish sneer is squatting down and taking various instruments out of a bag.

"I know what you mean," I say, because I see how the creature, needle by needle, awl by awl, jabs the child's belly and rubs shame's dye in with his fingers. And the belly's anointed with bitter bilberries. And tainted script on it up to the waist. And the tattoo artist hasn't even stood up before that jealous Arab, that Arab cuckolded by sailors, parts his silks and, pulling out his rosy little piglet, sprinkles that inscription, still fresh, with Arab urine till the little chap writhes with searing pain! But what of it—clog-danced by those lackeys to the ground . . . so he can't move hand or foot.

Thomas seizes his head in huge paws and shakes it. Once, twice. And sees that I'm bemused.

"You must know, Professor, kaleidoscope technique . . . I often use it, especially at tricky moments . . . Mechanical redeployment of theme. Radical method. You try."

"Why, of course," I respond quickly, seizing my head in both hands. Only rattling to be heard now. Walnuts in a pot. Scenes merge and fragment, no trace of Yazit, sheikh, and rabble. Just one lip of the cuckold Arab is left, and it's by no means clear how he managed it, but suffice it to say that with the one lip he succeeded in letting us know what this inscription means:

I Am A Whore I Give My Arse To All Comers

"My dear man," Thomas says to me, "let's try one more

time! Maybe some more cheerful picture will turn up?"

And once again our heads are two kaleidoscopes, all shivers and shudders. And we see that bunch holding Yazit, and the little boy has to swallow their brutality and blows standing up. They take stabs at him barrack-room style, rampaging like brute beasts.

"Look!" Thomas shouts proudly, pointing at something with his huge finger. Because viewed from another angle the infant Yazit's grown so glorious that two white peacocks have come down from the heavens and perched on him. And have turned violet!

"Like you, he loved his mother very much," says Thomas, "and as long as I remember him, he always used to send the old woman a tidy mite . . . a good son." (And Thomas smiles.) "Professor . . . there's no one here, so why don't you put your eye to my eye again . . . well? Don't be afraid. Like sooo. OK?"

I look into his eye, and there's a Parisian room under a grudging bulb. And all that's visible is the torso of a galloping Yazit, his dark chest rocking forward and then back. And the horse under him is pale in color. I seem to recognize it from somewhere. You can see the joy in Yazit's gaze at the collision of the two bodies. You can see the joy of this ride, as the young Berber's shouting something with a face already starting to screw up against the approaching storm. Swept along by this storm, Yazit freezes into a statue but still keeps on savaging, and, while making his kill, yells:

"Ruuudiii! Ruuuuu . . . "

I disengage, leaning toward Thomas.

"Who's he with there?"

"With me," says Thomas in an unusually gentle voice, "that's me . . . my second name is Rudolf. But it's my first for those, well, for . . . you know . . . my very own. Yazit, he's the only one . . . after Olek . . . who had the right to call me that."

I look at his two eyes, pale and smiling, and although I

don't go near them, I can hear in Tom-Rudolf's huge head how, round after round, the fight to the finish of gasping fuckers draws to a close. To the point where above us, here on the castle ceiling, the grapes grow shaggy with raven short hairs and start to belabor each other and jog in time to that double-bellowsed Parisian gasping.

A car's driven into the courtyard. We've glanced through the window. The windowpane has thawed and the sky's come into the dining room, combed by the comb of the cock perched on the day's last hill. It's stopped snowing. A coarse-grained air pinched our ears, and lights of houses some way off on neighboring hills reminded us abruptly of the vastness of this earth where people have already started to count the leaves on the calendar separating them from Christmas, the time when dreaming parts the snows to spill wolf and hare from the vellum of an unexpected greensward so that they can start to sing a two-part Manichaean carol about the birth of light, a carol without which we would walk even more blindly.

We were both aware that so many hours and worlds and lights had multiplied between us, it was best to utter words slowly as if, walking through a field of rye, we were pushing aside dreams of gray thread and diseased weeds with a gentle movement of our hands. He gave me his hand.

"Au revoir, Thomas," I said, squeezing his huge bony paw.

"Rudolf . . . Rudolf . . . ," he corrects me, "you're welcome to call me that . . . if you like the idea."

"Rudolf," I said. But articulating the word, I didn't know whether I was simply getting closer to a foreigner casually encountered in a Gold Market or, by the same token, taking a white horse by the bridle . . .

And even now, in the train, I really have to open my eyes wide so my head can let off steam through them. So as to belch sand through my eyes, sand that carries more and more traces of the heels of those Arabs and sailors fresh from Yazit. No one to see me. Hurry up! Stand here. I'll pay well. Yazit, Rudolf, the jealous Arab heading sailors starved by the voyage. And even the tattoo artist. I plant them in a row . . . And who's that I'm pushing in among them? That one over there in her grammar-school uniform. Get on, lads! And they look at each other, who's to go first. And see that I've made a fan of dollars and am fanning myself with it . . . And by this time they're getting the idea. Already each man's taken his smoked bacon in the hollow of his hand. And there's nothing but a seething whirlpool. From hand to groping hand she flies. They're tearing her uniform off with their teeth so as not to extract, not to distract their hands from her. Now the tattoo artist rushes her viciously, so brutally that even the sailors pull back appalled, as they've never seen such butchery! And the girl sweeps the meadow of glaring buttercups with her gray-goose braids. And the tattoo artist's got hazel eyes. And shouts in Polish: "That's for the pony you tortured to death!" Loud applause from the assembled company as if to stress the justice and unanimity of the charge.

I'm throwing banknotes to the crowd. Hurling themselves on the money, they raise such a cloud of sand that only Rudolf's head, huge as a hot-air balloon, escapes the hurricane. And is convulsed with laughter, licking a great senile finger withdrawn from a dished-up chicken. Even some dirty old man I don't know blinks his eyes, licking a little vanilla boy impaled on his claw.

And above all this floats the sheet-metal noise of the train clattering through the middle of the night like an honest gray on a track scattered with silver oats. And at this moment in time nobody hears the men-pike, six feet tall, as they prowl the valley, bespattered to the spine with the blood of roaches that form a flattering guard of honor for these condottieri created in the image and likeness of the King of Kings.

This billowing sky above the Kraków marketplace, this actual and material sky across which the wind's setting clouds afloat, brings relief. And the puff of air that lifts the tablecloths on the little tables in front of the Cloth Hall isn't even irritating. All you have to do is merge these phenomena into your existence, these pigeons, say, that dawdle round the square like silly hens then soar once more like doves full of pearly theology, so that the day may seem worthy of time in eternity.

The selfsame part played by picture postcards lying right here in front of the sugar bowl, full of their everlasting skies, flaunting their diminutive size in a suspect manner like a female circus dwarf in silks and sequins. On her back, which is to say on the back of St. Mary's tower, on the back of the Cloth Hall, I inscribe hieroglyph words, striving for wit and aptness. But all at once the sun's blotted out. And a thousand tourists look up to the sky, their attention fixed on that child star running behind a fence, behind a fence, behind a fence—look!—it's run out now and is smiling from ear to ear again.

My own feigned foreignness confronting this town that doesn't remember me. A donning of white gloves so as to impress upon the tempo of this place my own elegance and unhurried air that says: "In a minute, in a minute . . . I'm under no obligation to fly like the clouds, as the wind blows."

But what is my obligation? I must keep transmitting thoughts from here to our Mam and Thomas, and through Thomas to Yazit, who's already only a picture postcard scribbled over with whips and so forth . . .

And I must listen to today's bands converging from factories and suburbs for the inauguration of a memorial. I feel as though they're hemming me in with sheet-metal notes, with urgent muttering of drums, so that I'm sitting here with Yazit and Thomas in the guise of a bouquet of everlasting flowers smelling of mice, continually sipping European coffee and looking at my European ballpoint.

Meanwhile, the bands come closer and closer, battering and clashing their cymbals. By now these cymbals are shields! And it's like a march for the drums and martial for the flutes squealing in something approaching Turkish style. But my ballpoint's a ballpoint still. The historicity of the morning's given body by schools, scout troops, coachloads of workers (with their own booze in the luggage compartment). Hordes of children beat time with their feet where they're standing. Even gray-haired citizens of my vintage start marking time with their feet, forgetful of the woodworm in their peg legs. Why, by now even that woodworm's humming "And did those feet in ancient time" to its maple leg. And my ballpoint's heating up. I'm left here on my own, because everyone's followed the bands, jumping in the air to snap shots of the parade, so as to snatch these heads enrolled for an anniversary day like potatoes all set for popping into a large dish embellished with a lavish spoonful of May butter, so as to trap them in time and then stow this time away in a drawer with a view to honorable rancidity and the annual fry-up of the beefsteak kept under an old-style Uhlan cavalry saddle.

I'm sitting alone and the waitresses keep looking at me with resentful periwinkle eyes, as no doubt they'd have closed the café, and in windblown tablecloths, scattering sugar from silver casters, drinking toasts in Coca-Cola champagne, they'd have marched . . . Vivat! after the lads impersonating scythe-bearing Polish rebels of two hundred years back, who are hurriedly stuffing their jeans in their boot legs so as to turn themselves into those authentic peasant heroes and are setting off in farmcarts full tilt after the procession, cracking their whips rock and roll style . . .

But everything's eluding my grasp. All at once I feel like a student finalist waiting in the corridor. But there are still hurried clouds above my head and architecture emptied of people all around. I get up and set off, boosting my morale by swinging my arms vigorously, in the direction of St. Mary's cathedral. I twist round on impulse: not even a trace of my passing. As if no one had passed that way. And yet I remember . . .

To go inside, if only for a moment. Because after all, "Drop in, since you're there, see where your parents got married . . . in the church of Mary. Maybe you'll call to mind something like a paternoster, you rascal you." An expanse of dark brick, high as the vault under my granny's warm black skirt when she'd stand at the well drawing water that had sunk in the hot weather. Twirls of time round our Mam's spindle. Like a well-controlled thread, like a gray strand, I twist round—turn in a circle—shrink . . . Out into the sun!

And over there where the crowds have gathered, the bands have suddenly gone quiet. The people must have sighed, because that sigh's run right up to me, a rustle of sound, and enveloped me in a flowery kerchief, a canvas hood, a striped Łowicz skirt, stitchwort, so that I lengthen my stride and don't run but career as if chasing my kite across country, across the potato field, letting my cap fly away, letting the landowner loose his dog after me—just as long as I can catch my white and red Polish eagle, which is making a bid for its first skies on a child's thread . . . But for God's sake . . . a wall of people! I've gotten bogged down in pensioners. In old men who haven't had the strength to squeeze deeper into the inaugural throng and stand here, catching scraps of the speech which a compassionate wind brings to them, a bit chewed up and partially digested.

Suddenly, silence. And straight after it a distant clanking, now nearer, a rattling, rumbling, grumbling, clattering fills Kraków now right up to the hurrying clouds. I clutch my ballpoint—because it's my Europeanness—because it won't let me turn myself into a gawker at the Częstochowa shrine, but here's a little old man, stifled and purple with asthma, pointing at the sky for me. "Look," he wheezes. And my nape positively aches with the determination not to look up. I don't hold out. I'm looking.

From the skies to the south, no doubt from warmer climes,

a monstrous thrumming object's gliding, gleaming with metal and slowly hauling over us a golden cargo, King Jagiełło on his horse. And while all this is dangling threateningly in the air—the bells strike up their own rhythm. In deserted churches organists-cum-bell ringers throw themselves on the ropes—with both hands, with the whole of their body down to the stone floor! And now they fly up, right up under the vaulting, but sins of the flesh and heavy drinking pull them back to earth. Nonetheless, towers have already been set asway. And already Kraków's waist deep in clerical Latin and episcopal mumbling. So much so that the provincial party secretary orders a statement on the radio to the effect that this doesn't count.

But I stand here among the pensioners and search for a happy medium between their toothless bliss and my supreme independence that's without rhyme or reason. And while I go on pretending that I'm forcing myself to stand there and be one of the crowd—a sudden burst of applause over there, positive cascades of bravos because the Party secretary's given a sign to heaven with his hand and at once the flying chaff-chopper starts to descend along with the Lithuanian king of Poland made fast by a chain of office. Already his provincial nag, translated into the bronze of a monumental charger by courtesy of Silesian metalworkers, touches the pedestal with its four hooves. Already the king's looking the shops over with a wily eye, wanting to weigh the honor or dishonor of his statue status here against their super- or nonabundant stock. That's that. He's in position. So a march, a mazurka, and we're all made of bronze! And cymbals go up over heads, gilded to pancakes. And they're at it again! And it's over. And the pensioners make for doorways in fright—because the population's going back to the town center and is apt to trample them underfoot. Thousands of feet across the market square. Sour Lithuanian rye soup in restaurants. Even the black-market currency dealers swear because all at once they're robbed of room to maneuver in bars crowded with brothers-in-arms celebrating the king's victory at Grünewald five hundred years ago.

It's gone quiet. At last I can come out of this doorway. Once again the people of this place will have the chance of observing me from a distance. Tree-lined Planty Avenue is its tree-lined self once more, the trees stand erect, but in spite of this there's a certain feeling of incipient grave-yardage. As if this explosion of pride, oratory, and musicians' bulging cheeks, as if all this has been swept into a black sack reigned over by Queen Naphthaline of the moth-balls. A sense of incipient pastness. Skirting empty trampled ice-cream tubs and bronchial spittle, I go up to the monu-ment. And here's a stench of gladioli, carnations, sunflowers, vying in fading, of sprays and wreaths delegations have laid round the plinth and even round the hooves of the royal mount so that it might "drown in flowers." Already flies have made a start on the stuff. Other than them, only I am mobile. First I'll walk round the square as if I'm a tourist, as if I want to look at it from a suitable angle, as if I'm one of those who screw up their faces, crouch down, shift the sun behind them, order an orphan to cry poignantly—*but* when this sort's taking a shot, then just you feast yourself on it! Wave after wave of competitors borrows your little orphan so that before they give her back to you the model will have moved from orphanage to old people's home.

But this king what's-his-name, how this *gut-bag* slumps in his saddle, satisfied that the people of Kraków have endowed him with a not-unreasonable square footage in return for the Grünewald victory. You'll see . . . he'll be opening a kiosk here for himself yet, with pickled cucum-bers, and hire out his tatty steed to big-bellied expats . . . I'll stand closer up, why not in the statue's own shadow come to that? Hmm . . . there's a foursquare brainpan for you . . . with a head like that he'd have been a cook in Auschwitz by rights . . . Hmm . . . a dog wouldn't be amiss just now . . . two, three, five dogs so as to . . . piddle till it's pouring! A regular pool . . . but he'd think it's the dew. His own horse would burst out snickering! And . . . just suppose you were to bribe church pigeons with corn, lure them here in a flock, if only for one little hour so that they'd spatter the horse a dreary gray. So they'd simply coat him with edelweiss from heaven!

What's that? All at once Jagiełło starts to creak alarmingly, wrestling with the metals in his saddle, gnashing bronze teeth against each other and clashing against his horse's crupper with his unwieldy sword! On the crupper with the flat of the blade! Giddyap! Until the horse prizes itself painfully off its pedestal.

But I don't wait to see which way the wind's blowing. By this time I'm away, fucking off straight across country till my foreign loafers pummel me with their heels. And Jagiełło's very close, spitting mad, but he's afraid of little alleyways, he's bowling along on the asphalt hurling tarred and feathered oaths after me like a peasant-rogue. Wait— I've got an idea—and hey presto! into the Barbican. And I'm running inside the bastion like the proverbial mouse while he clangs with his sword on the outer wall till it rings so my ears are splitting and I'm pawing at my head. And I'm so deafened that I make a sally, come what may. But he does nothing. He leans against the Barbican and butts me in the back with his laugh, uncouth laughter unworthy of matriculation, so hearty that it's thrown me into the marketplace. I still shout at him: "Lithuanian duke, you make lice puke." But he only stamps, horse and man, on the pavement with the result that I've lost my equilibrium in this earthquake and fall flat.

But in no time someone's hands pull me firmly to my feet, and fleetingly, right next to my face, I see first tufts of corn-colored hair, then young eyes under a Kraków costume hat pushed down defiantly over a nose. Because when I fell, blown over by the king, a quadrille of those scythe-carrying insurrectionists was just passing through the square. Hidden in ambush behind a polyester haystack, fellows from television were filming this rococo folksiness and directing changes in the figures of the dance with sudden handclaps. The one who'd picked me up didn't have a scythe. He had scraps of paper in his hand with the text of his heroic role's oath.

"Hand him over, chief!" the insurrectionists began shouting. "To the dance with him!"

And before I know it I'm already thrust forward, held under the armpits, absorbed by the insurrectionists. At the same time, scytheless. A ballpoint isn't a scythe, and each of them's holding his own like a holy candle by its butt. And puffs out his chest in a sprightly fashion, first his boots, then his teeth gleaming toward the camera. And so we string our legs along. They look at me, and I, albeit your anachronistic civilian, try as best I can to stretch a pastoral smile under my nose, but suddenly my Parisian Saint-Laurent tie gets hooked up on my neighbor's scythe—and chop! a tiny bow tie, bob-tailed like a blackbird chick. But I keep on leaping all the same, rather amused by this incident. But now the insurrectionist on my right—hop! squashes the shiny tip of my soft shoe with his folksy clog. Never mind. By this time I don't feel so tense; I'm even executing pirouettes with my trouser leg and holding my ballpoint away from me at arm's length like they do their scythes. Even the woman selling white roses looks benignly at me and nods her head maternally. And my companions, too, as though they've started to believe in me, as though my heroic foreignness coming over to their side had convinced them.

I do this Marketplace folk dance for them, but I'm dancing more and more for myself as well. And I feel how my gamboling's more pleasing than their routine, of more value because it's out of the common run. So I make fresher efforts till a fellow from television sticks his thumb in the air as a sign that he's never seen such a cracking Krakowian.

After this dancing, beer. We sat down on the pavement. It turned out that the insurrectionist brotherhood was from the State Acting School. Their historic chief Kościuszko taps me on the shoulder and says:

"I can see, mate, that you've really got into the feel . . . Apropos—I've actually got a scythe at home straight from the Polish-Russian battlefield, you know, from old Racławice . . . a practically genuine old relic! You clean it up a bit with Brasso and it'll shine for you in the West . . . and some vicious bite it's got! It'll rip open—swissh! a letter from your girl . . . I'm getting ready to go over to your part of the world, hitching a lift, you'll be sure to find me some beat-up Volkswagen there, where you live the ditches are full of this scrap iron, OK?"

And everyone gets up, including me. And they start to go down in a line like geese to the underground lavatory so as to get rid of their beer. But I don't. I stand in the middle of the Marketplace in my gaping shirt and see that the flower seller's wiping tears away with the hem of her nylon apron. I go up to her. And point to the white roses. She doesn't want to take money. I kiss her on both hands. And she kisses me on the head.

And with the flowers that have taken root very nicely in place of my tie, I move on slowly across the square. I raise my eyes. In the sky a file of storks in national colors. They string along so languidly that they don't really need to use wings. I turn off into Planty Avenue. What's this? Chestnut trees, as if scorched by summer already, are scattering their stereotyped leaves liberally over a pensioner, so appropriate for this season of autumn. I reach the monument. Quiet here and leaves up to the knees. A road sweeper turns and brushes clockwise. King and horse are at home like the sweeper and his tool of local birch twigs. But I? I want to search for something, I'm groping through my pockets with a slow hand, turning them inside out, but by this time I can't even remember what it was or wasn't.

And with pockets open to the breeze, with docked tie, I don't walk but wobble toward the station on my graying childhood scooter. And suddenly a guard of honor, children, grown-ups, and old folk. Drawn up by generation. They give friendly shouts, and I tear petals off the roses and throw them, and as I'm throwing, all at once I notice rotten wood and vermin scattering from my scooter in all directions so that the ground's reddish. So I begin to stamp, to tread it all underfoot, but they think this is my famous insurrectionist dance with a pinch of expat Polonization. A deluge of bravos. So I really do dance and turn to steel because of the flashbulbs, they take so many shots of me, and after a last bout of stamping I throw my arms wide like any hero, in the shape of a cross. And I actually have to shut my eyes because of the blast of cries and applause.

Our Mam must be watching television now, and tears will be flowing from her gray eyes.

Rudolf was waiting for me at the end of one of the streets, leaning on a bench. Catching sight of me, he slowly raised his hand. Still a dozen paces or so. We open our mouths, adjust our smiles.

Good—by now we've gotten over RSVP initial greetings, emotions and surprises. We've been sitting for some minutes on a concrete bench fixed to the wall of a ten-story building bearing the name D.11, so proud a name that if it weren't for the laundry on the corner, if it weren't for the beer house and its resident cripple, I'd never have found this D.11.

Rudolf's holding his hands on his knees. It's as though the skin on his face has grown in volume, especially under the eyes. He's listening and signaling agreement. He doesn't have this sort of visit often, for sure. And the people who pass us exchanging *Guten Tags* with him seem to be congratulating him on such a guest. I tell my story while he looks at me as if King Jagiełło had endowed me with silver and amber, as if he wanted to peck the pearliness of the Kraków pigeons out of my eyes, as if he wanted to tear from my mouth the drawled vowels shaped by the muzzles of the lads who'd given themselves up to the rhythm of the dance on the Marketplace that time in front of the camera. But when I put my hands on my knees for a moment, his gaze comes to rest on them, and he says with a smile:

"I can see you carried your hands behind you, as befitted a professor . . . and so they're not sunburned."

I looked at my hands. They lay next to his laborer's paws, really much paler. His, in spite of rust-colored blotches and wrinkling and veins, were clinging to his knees like speckled toads so as not to fall. While mine had alighted like cerebral butterflies . . .

"That's because of gloves," I say. "You know, it's chancy over there when it comes to hygiene . . . "

And I begin to rub my hands, not because it's cold but to stop him from inspecting them so intently.

"You were keeping your hands behind your back . . . you can only catch hold of the past that way . . . *et encore* . . . Please don't be hard on a pensioner who's become peevish, but . . . to spend a holiday in your native land wearing gloves . . . in summer . . . it's like fondling someone through an overcoat."

I look at his hands, his down-at-heel shoes that he was wearing way back, that time in the gilded Grand'Place in Brussels. I smile and reply:

"Rudolf . . . I haven't struggled for thirty years here in the West, getting together property and prestige so as to . . . start slumming over there . . . They—you know—over there they only appreciate possessions . . . and heroics . . . Every second fellow takes one look at my hair and asks me about *the war* on the spot. And after five minutes it turns out we got the same snow down our collars during roll call at Auschwitz, that we cured our dreams in the crematorium smoke . . . And so on and so on, shuffling the ashes of companions onto a couple of spades, counting little corpses that used to whistle tangos along with us, pinch and munch apples with us . . . But gloves," I go on, "they're a leap into another civilization . . . You should have seen how respectfully they treated me there in the Marketplace . . . they invited me into the front row at the unveiling . . . Over there everyone wants to squeeze a hand just like this one in white, rose-pink, or sky-blue gloves, and they're beside themselves in no time if there's an American label on the glove . . . "

"I know what you mean . . . I know what you mean," says Rudolf in a low voice, and signals with his smile that presumably everything's been said on this matter.

"I don't know if you do quite know what it all means," I retort, "because over there I get a bit like an archaeologist . . . You know . . . wherever I turn—a plaque with an epitaph or a crucifix at a road junction. You can't avoid them. You have to make a detour. You wave your hand about to show it's nonsense, but here's your hand so swamped in waving that you've got to rescue it like a drowned man . . . And people stare at your struggles . . . But white gloves now, these tombstones were still in awe of them, as you might say."

Having said this, I place my hands on my knees again. Let him gaze his fill now.

But he's closed his eyes and is enjoying the sun, breathing and nodding his head thoughtfully like that time when he was leaving the Grand'Place in his pensioners' coach.

"I know what you mean . . . I know what you mean," he whispers.

"I don't know . . . You're always ready with your 'I-know-what-you-mean-I-know-what-you-mean,' but to start with you've got to see it really to grasp it. The people have been walled in with graves, and they're nothing more than deep-gold tench going from dam to dam . . . and they fatten themselves on the slime of the past. I took my gloves off at the frontier . . . "

Rudolf, looking straight in front of himself, turned to me. You could see words had already come swimming up to his mouth, but he was still waiting, maybe picking, choosing among those words, till finally:

"You took them off . . . but here and there weren't they

red, along with the skin they'd grown to?" He's flicked an eye at his watch. "Maybe we'll take a short stroll . . . we'll drop into a café . . . over there on the terrace opposite . . . because there's a painter in my flat, unluckily: paints and drafts."

We're going toward some D— or other along a slippery pavement, slippery as your soles after leaving a forest of pine needles. Rudolf's breathing heavily. I stop as if I want to ask about something, what's that building over there in some shitty dead end or other. And he, kindhearted fellow, pretends he's taking my question seriously and says:

"It's a theater . . . but I've never been there," and suddenly he starts to laugh in that way he has, shamelessly. "That's something absolutely right for Poles . . . I was listening to your tale and thinking to myself . . . these Poles, they behave as though every single one of them, without exception, spent his life on horseback . . . But on horseback, all you can do is give orders, knock Turks' heads off with your saber to add flavor to Viennese coffee, but you can't lower your pants either in front or behind. You can't use your body except for carrying a standard, lance, or holy images . . . You thought you'd skive off from your horse in your white gloves . . . and instead you've come back from the old place more cavalry than infantry, you've grown like a mummer's mask that scatters horse's neighs across a December night, but down below your peasant's gaiters go wading village-style through the snow . . . left-right, left-right . . . Let's sit down here."

He's turned to face D.II. Some woman's just come out in front of the building. He looks me in the eye. Several species of gargantuan laughs and chuckles are chasing across his pupils. He's thinking up something for sure, he's working on it. He's got it. But he's still lapping coffee.

"You know . . . I believe in riding too. The African continent really thundered under us when I mounted Yazit . . . But when he'd stretch me at full gallop, spur and goad me on—to the point where Paris began to heel over! Man! Cavalry times!"

And he sketches a circle in the air with his hand as if he were throwing a lasso at the sun . . .

And laughs at his own histrionics. He's turned serious. He drinks coffee and his eyes grow melancholy, nine-teenth-century eyes. The daredevil's mellowed. He's mellowed and words come from behind the coffee steam:

"Maaan, it's over. You've seen those rides of mine, that I sent you . . . I was a devil of a lad then . . . you hear . . . and today—I'm a pensioner, a granddad after his second heart attack . . . And my green tattoo's covered with senile cataract. You're still young . . . try to escape. Try to leap clear of your horse while there's time, run to some alder stream, throw off all your worldly trappings, step into the water . . . And before you know where you are, some shepherd will be washing your head, shoulders, and back, so that all of a sudden you'll see the meaning of water, birds, light, and broth-erhood *with your body!*"

He fell silent, but his Frühlingsmarsch was still going on around us, hacked out despairingly by cymbals entangled in a spider's web of clouds going to mange for good and all.

After each meeting with Rudolf, after each letter from him, it was as if I was forced to stoop and shift aside the next stone on the path, the next slab, so as to expose the white guts of darkness twisting and turning as prey for light. When for no particular reason his impudent laugh breaks out without warning, my head's racing mad, ready to go for his ear with an argument, but not a bit of it . . . my thoughts froth like beer badly poured into a pint pot so that in no time over my forehead, out of my ears, and down the back of my neck maggots stream out, never to reach the pupa stage.

Our Mam knows the pickle I'm in. It upsets her that a German, even though he's well-disposed and respectable, is tormenting me so.

"After all, you are a professor," she writes. "Say something to him, that old Teutonic knight, put him with his back to the wall, make him reel, then he will give you some peace."

"It is not so easy where he is concerned," I explain. "You know, Mam . . . he always tosses a stronger card on the table. He says it is just men among men who are up to such unheard-of things, you know, as the ones I told you about that time."

A good month went past. A letter. The beginning like a beginning: "You know, they caught that cow who was pinching dollars out of American letters. You knew her father, people are scared that he is going to hang himself . . . " Then about the river that's turbid, about the trucks that raise dust and keep hooting as well, but at the end a post-script: "When you are here in a month's time, I have something for you, something our granny that is gone used to tell me. You see, I was going to take this beastly thing with me to the grave, but this way you can make yourself mucky with it, too. You wanted to, yourself."

July had forgotten about air. You simply breathed rainwater fermenting in a barrel along with an apiary radiating bees' venom so it burned your throat! Across a heavy sky swarms of bees kept passing each other, hustling, buzzing toward forests full of hollow trees. Look—this very minute—a mouse thief's falling onto the base of a hive, crawling in its death agony, stabbed by stings and growing stiff, embalmed . . .

In the middle of August, when I'd sat down in the prewar deck chair and gorged myself on wild strawberries drenched with cream in a little pot I remember from over fifty years back, our Mam took out a small cardboard file and began to leaf through papers.

"Dog's . . . dinner! I'm dead certain that creature next door's pinched it off me . . . you know, I had a nice picture postcard, from those very same foreign parts . . . "

She sat down next to me but got up at once.

"Shall we have a drink, the two of us? Not home brew, don't fret . . . "

Then, when we were licking vodka-seasoned lips, our Mam, begins like this:

"You remember that nice glass dish?"

"The one that old woman next door got from you in '39, Mam, with fritters for her saint's day, and didn't give back?"

"That's the one . . . You remember she had a son who was a priest, and she'd go to confession every day, but used to hit her servant girl on the snout so that a fresh one was forever running away each month?"

"I remember . . . so what . . . "

"Hang on. She was forever seeing the neighbor with the little billy-goat's beard had a way of dropping in here, to have a bit of fun . . . "

"Poptiu?"

"Poptiu . . . And just you imagine, that old death's-head . . . whether for envy or whatever, it boils down to her sitting down one day on the steps by the door and starting like this: 'Poptiu's asked me round on his saint's day, but I shan't go.' She stops and looks at me. And I look at her and say nothing, because I've had an arseful of this. But she—you know—smiles smarmily: 'I've tangled once with him already' . . . And she stops again. And I still don't say anything. 'You know,' she says, 'he'd often go off to a little town up there in the mountains and give us a lift from time to time, now me, now my daughter, up to the presbytery to see my son. Same thing this time. It was Sunday. There'd been such a downpour during the night you couldn't sleep. And in the morning people came to church covered with so much mud that gravel scrunched all over the church floor. In the marketplace, as if for spite, not a single cart from my son's village. I come back home and here in Poptiu's yard there's a cart covered with tarpaulins. Is he going? He's going. Of course there's room. Well then, the peasant's in the driving seat up front, and we're in the back. At every bend, Poptiu's got me by the waist "so I wouldn't fall." I still had on—you know—that nice black skirt for church—but he wants to shove his great paws up. "Dirty pig," I say, "lay off, your wife that's paralyzed is praying at home now . . . and you . . . " But you know yourself the way he is! Well then, we drive out of town. And our road's—you know— right by the river. And the river's risen so high that the whole valley's awash with yellow water. But that blighter's having it off in his head. I push him away, but I've got to hold onto the cart's wicker lining so as not to tumble out head over heels. What's more, I've got to look after my black straw hat, in case it falls off. And he's swelled up like a bull at stud. You know what a big head he's got . . . And suddenly, it's even bigger . . . As big as this! And nothing but puffing and panting from it. And chuckling and enormous teeth. And all at once—if I'd had any warning—he kneels down in the hay, pushes me backward, grabs me under the knees, and tears off my drawers! And he thrusts his great tongue out of that demon-horse gob and he's at me . . . you know . . . a carpenter's rasp! But I seize him by the hair so as not to fall off the bench. And pull. What's the use. He doesn't give way. And suddenly the wind gets up and—bless your heart—my hat's off! It's floating. I let out a shriek. The peasant on the driver's seat turns round, sees what's up, and giddyap! he lashes the horse again . . . But this old lunatic with his billy goat's head slurps and laps for all the world like a young porker in a corner of the trough. What could I do? I waited till he took his head out of there . . . Anyway, at least he paid for my hat.'"

Our Mam poured me some vodka.

"I had no idea that old woman next door . . . was so randy . . . "

"Are you surprised? She was a Wieliczka woman."

"From Wieliczka?? The salt mine?"

"Good grief . . . even today, you go to a wedding in Domaradz, and you'll hear" (and our Mam begins to hum):

"Our bridesmaids' boobs are so ruddy big
You can ride 'em to Wieliczka, jig, jig, jig."

"I don't get it . . . it sounds as if . . . "

Our Mam poured one for herself and drank it at a gulp. She looked at me anxiously but started to smile at once.

"Laddie . . . you know I pray for you and go to confession . . . but what I'm going to tell you I've never let on to anyone . . . even the priest. You were too small to know your granny really well . . . She knew lots of things. Strange women used to come and sit by the door . . . outsiders, from all over the place. She'd make them at home and not even ask their names. 'Don't you know her, Mam?' I'd ask . . . but Granny just said: 'When anyone's got that look in her eyes and speaks like she does—then there's no need to ask so much as a name.' And that was all.

"Only later, when I was carrying you, on a day when that blighter next door had to be beating her girl, because the screaming was something fearful . . . Granny shakes her head indignantly and says: 'For shame, that Wieliczka woman . . . '—I started to drag it out of her . . . Laddie, no one knows about this . . . Listen. You remember what a fat thing she was . . . the one next door . . . a right bag of lard! To cut a long story short, when she got married, no sign of a child for the first three years. You knew her old man, he often used to give you a złoty, but way back when he was young, too right, you couldn't fault him . . . he was a real man. But somehow, nothing doing. Till this time in the fourth summer—the lass next door's not there. She's vanished. 'She's gone to take the waters,' he says. Hmm . . . But in the meantime she's trotted off to an old midwife. She certainly paid up. And the old girl took her away to Bochnia because the salt baths are said to be good there. Maybe, maybe not . . . But listen to this. They fixed up leaving here so as to get there just as night was coming on. And not in the town but somewheres a good way out of town. And there are swamps and stagnant pools, fells full of marshy backwaters and wasteland so that it's a proper nightmare. 'Heck,' she said to Granny afterward, 'wherever you go:

scrub, thickets, wild duck, and reeds. But first one woman gets out of a cart here, then a second and a third, each face muffled up in a head-scarf so you won't know them. The driver whips up his horse and—get up!—he's bolted. And what's more he's hoicking with disgust, pshaaw! And only when it got really dark,' she says to Granny, 'some sort of old woman turned up among us with a scarf up to her eyes: "Out of them shoes." And we go after her, barefoot, through puddles and standing water, till she leads us under some kind of overhang . . . We're waiting for what will happen and she's counting us . . . she jabs each one in the left breast with her finger, and when she's counted up to thirty-two of us, she says: "Hang on to each others' hands and follow me."

"'No lantern, no path under foot, nothing but sand and gravel. And all of a sudden there's a chilly breath, a sort of underground feel of where no one lives. We're all of a shudder. We grab on to each others' hands more tightly. But by this time there's no gravel under our feet but a pile of scree. And you can feel, because your feet are running away with themselves, that we're going downhill. And now there's a smell of something like smoke. And the woman leading us begins to sing from somewhere round a corner, or it seems like it. But with such a wailing peasant way of singing . . . Us at the back only caught on to what she was singing the second time around:

> Earth's mother
> Earth's mother
> Lady none fairer,
> What's this you hinder?

> We go this road
> To the water,
> None holier
> None younger . . .
> Thaw and open
> Earth's mother!

Before light
Thrust through night
The Lady bore
The Child-wight.

Suffering—Maria!
Suffering—Maria!
Lay yourself open
Lady none fairer!

"'At first we didn't know,' says the old woman next door to your granny, 'if it was all right to sing. But that woman sets up such a wailing for us . . . so much tenderness in her voice, that we feel it's not right to leave it just to her. To start with, we join in with some of the words, getting bolder bit by bit, but by the seventh time we're supporting her . . . and by the eighth and ninth,' she says, 'we've tuned our voices to her wild one, and with a real full-blooded yell on our lips, we went down into an underground cavern . . . the Red Gallery, women call it there. And there's so much smoke,' she says, 'that you have to breathe fast. And suddenly everyone's speaking, whispering, praying . . .

"'Our guide had to drag us by our hands away from the fire to the rocks that the spring waters gush out of . . . We washed ourselves there . . . '

"And the old blighter didn't want to tell Granny any more."

"But that fire . . . after all, maybe Granny . . . "

Our Mam began to look pensive. She sighed. You could see she regretted being so frank. That she wanted to draw back from her treachery, but at the same time longed to offer a gift to her son, the likes of which no woman and mother, either before or after her . . .

"Our granny would say, but I don't know if she'd been there . . . that the old women there, gray-haired hags, used to burn all kinds of midsummer herbs—St. John's herbs—and that the ones on pilgrimage would run about in these fumes, round . . . "

"Round what?"

"Give over now, do! I don't know. I haven't been there, thank God . . . "

She fell silent and sighed.

" . . . The old woman's son, you know he's a curate, he's bookish, but a well-beefed blighter, like his mother! He doesn't even know that he was born thanks to those herbs, or salt springs! He'd tell his mother the priests had known for a long time about the goings-on under Wieliczka . . . But what's to be done . . . go down into an abandoned salt mine on your bottom in your cassock so as to drive the women out of there with a sprinklerful of holy water?! It was only during the Occupation . . . some kind of crank . . . a seminarist, you know the sort, pale with red pimples and glasses . . . got two hollow-legged miners drunk and roped them together . . . And they led him down underground there."

"And . . . he found . . . the shit of the Holy Father carved into slices!"

"He found, laddie, he found . . . an image of the black Madonna . . . Very old . . . like a split oak! And enormous . . . But white at the base, for all that . . . hewn out of salt . . . with holes in it."

"Just a moment . . . what was that?"

"Weeell . . . the women . . . each of them wanted, you know . . . so that . . . well . . . through and through her."

"God help us, that I don't understand."

"Because you weren't listening to what they were singing. You go and ask Poptiu in his grave . . . He knew in the cart. Pour me another."

I poured one for myself, too. I stared straight in front of me.

"And that seminarist, Mam?"

"That seminarist . . . ran out of that hole—they used to say—like a scalded cat. And all fouled up like some ungodly monster!"

"But that image?! What became of that image?"

"The image . . . they pushed it over, the three of them,

into the pool by the spring. They poked it into the water with poles."

"And the seminarist? What happened to him?"

"He's sitting in a parish somewhere . . . near Lublin. An old man by this time." (She smiled.) "He wanted to be a bishop, used a lot of elbow, it was dreadful . . . but seemingly he turned out too nervy—the old woman's son used to say—you know, at the Elevation . . . the blighter was forever sprinkling his shoes with wine, his hands shook so!"

"And what does he call himself?"

"Give over, for pity's sake. I don't know . . . Reż . . . Żer . . . Żyr . . . Rżychiewicz . . . something like that."

If it weren't for the nightjars scattered across the Franciscan monastery on the skyline, we wouldn't even have noticed that twilight was creeping up on our eyes. Down below there was a smell of sweet resins on plum-tree bark scorched by the heat. Our Mam took me by the hand.

"Laddie . . . when you shut your Teutonic knight's mouth with what you've heard now . . . just say you read it in some old newspaper . . . OK? Because it's women's business . . . "

"All right, Mam."

While I was kissing her hand she was stroking my head. In the middle of the caress I sensed she was checking up on the size of my bald patch, as well as on the presence of two fatty lumps.

And the time in which we were floating suddenly hollowed out into the funnel of a whirlpool and began to hum like a bomb crater lined with musical bronze. So that even without Easter bells, space was both resurrected and echoed last things.

"No—no . . . there are mothers and mothers. You must get to know mine, Rudolf. Now don't look so surprised. Our Mam knows you very well from my stories . . . "

Rudolf somehow couldn't cope with a tiny smile which, like a moth frightened by sudden light, was fluttering now here, now there, and falling into every wrinkle round a mouth intent on the choice of words.

"But . . . really? To tell the truth, I suppose I know your mother pretty well, too, by now . . . from your stories . . . "

"I can't help wondering what flowers you'll appear on her doorstep with. Because it's very important."

"You're down to details already . . . but the matter still . . . I have no idea . . . well . . . isn't so very pressing, is it?"

"It most certainly is pressing . . . *I* shall advise you. In your place I'd bring carnations. White. You'll be asking, no doubt, why white carnations. You know . . . our Mam was and still is fond of the marriageability of things . . . You know . . . she brought a child up to manhood, she's buried a husband, but in spite of this she's kept this kind of . . . "

"Outrageous faith in the happiness of her nearest and dearest."

"Yyyes," I looked at him with astonishment, but he pretended he was trying to see past me, "that's why I think those carnations would be suitable."

"No. They wouldn't be suitable. I'd bring your mother roses . . . from a butcher, you know, flesh and blood—the kind of bouquet you can really fell an ox with."

Our Mam is sitting eyeless by the window, beyond which her wisdom from over the years spreads far and wide. She reaches out a hand to feel the waves of air and would seem to be waiting for something. The sparrows have noticed this, and they're off along the street to glean an ear of wheat . . . and what they glean . . . they pour onto that palm till it's engrained with these Lilliputian harvests . . .

The rain notices the palm. Remembers it, too. Remembers how this palm used to scoop it up with a sensual arm from a barrel that pulsed with the smell of Sodom and

Gomorrah, sulfurous after barely extinguished thunderbolts. And the rain pours itself onto her hand. Until not wheat but *oats* rise from the sparrows' grains and lick the old sun with a hundred tiny tongues. And there's a Polish Easter growing green with its oats. And there the traditional Lamb blossoms in blood.

"Mam," I say, "Rudolf would sit down here, here on the plush sofa . . . but before, when he came in, he'd give you eau de cologne, Mam . . . At least, that's what he was telling me . . ."

"Blow him and his prickly water . . . when you were little, you used to talk like that . . . but I'd rather clink glasses and drink schnapps with him, good schnapps, guzzle good smoked sausage, have a real belly laugh . . . I tell you, he could still be converted to women . . . and from what you say—he must be a smashing chap to have visit. You know, I picture him like a burgomaster. 'Whatever's got out? Why it's beer and sauerkraut' . . . You know, he's got something in common with a butcher here . . . you didn't know him . . . you were little . . . When I used to go to that butcher's, he'd wrestle so hard with the meat on his counter, knife it and slice it so hard . . . that I used to stand there and couldn't tear my eyes away from it . . . Your father didn't like him, when he used to come to us to kill a young pig, said he was 'a brute' . . . Poor old dad . . . as if you could shove a knife into a pig, holding the thing between two fingers . . . I see this Rudolf of yours as a butcher."

"But Mam, you were saying . . . he was a burgomaster."

"What are you after? . . . Stop going on at me . . . a butcher, not a burgomaster. But suppose maybe—well, a butcher for a burgomaster! There!"

Rudolf is looking at the photograph.

"My beloved professor . . . the photographer's ordering your mother to stand rigid here because this portrait's from the days when you weren't allowed to move . . . but I see your mother running to the river . . . and rather than look at the water, she's gazing at her breasts, how they bump themselves against her, how they dance a jig. And she bursts out laughing . . . I swear to you . . . Just like my Olek . . . a wild beach in Brittany, empty as evening's coming on . . . I tell you, you just had to see him as he ran to the sea . . . with everything jigging that felt a part of himself, till he laughed like your mother."

And Rudolf starts to laugh with the help of those two other laughs, which he dominates like a station supervisor— the frightful old woodpecker. He actually snorts with their selfsame impudence.

"Professor dear . . . men build memorials to weeping and wounds but . . . who's going to set up a public monument to laughter? . . . I'd chisel a huge pumpkin in alabaster, hollowed out, full of horrible primitive eyes and teeth . . . so that whoever wanted to could put a candle inside and summon up from the darkness laughter as carnivalesque and subversive . . . as a naked arse."

And he actually doubles up in a fresh bout of laughter at the sight of the monument that, with the eyes of a seventy-year-old kid, he's charmed from imperial Byzantine alabaster into a dangling, scatological Chinese lantern . . .

To rub a five-groszy transfer with a spit-wetted finger, to wet and rub again at the left-hand side of the world, tearing off paper shrouds behind which reality's waiting for us, still damp from that miraculous spittle with which we opened its eyes.

To breathe on windowpanes frosted with the lime of death so as to catch a glimpse of a dawn frozen to the marrow. To set out toward that dawn, picking out from its color—flowers and lips . . . or fire and slaughter?

The need to march out beyond the tollgates onto common land where the sand of indifference is piled. Church bells and police whistles don't reach as far as here, where a dog with a lame leg looks at you in silence because he knows no one will snarl back at him there.

As far as the river. Pull that child's carriage out of the slime and go with it, straight ahead. Already inside it, Rudolf's head, two feet wide, and Poptiu's bull mug, baring its teeth in an impudent chuckle, and our Mam's head full of eyes where faded jackdaws chatter.

My dear laddie,

I have not been out for a month, as what is the use? So I can look for people by groping in a game of blindman's buff? Oh, I was forgetting, a chap from television was here, you know, you danced with them . . . They want to invite you to dance again. He said they will pay. What is more, you will be on television. And although I will not see it, I shall still find out from people: "Missus, I saw your son, he was dancing the krakowiak." More likely, I shall pop off before you come. Remember to plant a nice fern on my grave. God forbid dahlias, because they smell like rotten potatoes after the first frost. But a fern now, it will get rust-colored in winter, that is true, but it will stay dry and parchmentlike. And later the snow will cover it up nice and neatly, so that it is drifted over. On the other hand, in May—I do not have to describe to you how it will give itself airs . . . People when they pass that way (and you, too, you rascal, when you come to your mother's grave to pray), they will say: "Look, do look how that old blighter has dolled herself up!"

"Now professor," says Rudolf, "leave that carriage alone with its three heads. You've got mutilated bodies all over again . . . A man doesn't dream just with his head . . . "

And he wants to lift his shirt up once more to show me the tattoo. So I get in first and say:

"With his head . . . with his head . . . battered and bruised . . . but with his head. Listen . . . " (and I sense that my voice is turning Slav) " . . . Day had just dawned, freezing, when the Germans evacuated us from Gross-Rosen . . . squeezed into railway trucks like cattle. We're on our way . . . But you can hear something reverberating already . . . the gunfire of Red Army batteries . . . And suddenly . . . some sixteen-year-old Russian lad, blackened with hunger, grabs me by the arm and bawls above the groaning of the trucks: '*Palyak, slushay, Katyusha payot!* Pole, listen, the rocket launcher's singing, Katyusha's singing!'—and he's shaking with wet-eyed laughter. Rudolf . . . you know about the fern . . . winter turns it rusty, but the time comes when a crosier will raise itself from the cold earth and begin to uncurl, so as to burst into glory on Midsummer Night, St. John's Night, with all its treasures. As long as I've got a memory, this little Russian . . . my dear man . . . those four words that he blurted out . . . I carry them inside me, and they'll keep on rising up in me from under the misery and deprivation of those years that were louse-bitten by God's own louse."

Rudolf was keeping his hands on the table. They lay like toads with their heads shattered by a stick, speckled with scabby blotches of red. He kept on listening to my silence for some time and then raised his eyes.

"Professor . . . I know what you mean. I feel it in my bones . . . but it wasn't *that* I had in mind . . . it was more . . . that all our heads have been inoculated with this cult of public mutilation and death on the barricades . . . and so on from generation to generation. It's reached a point where the head, drunk with heroic hysteria, gazes 'with pride' and 'with self-denial' . . . at the despair of the body that nourishes it . . . So that when the body falls, the head's still reciting that select number of little verses, you know, that force you to stand to attention automatically . . . "

"These heads . . . my dear chap . . . when they're capable of gritting their teeth . . . sometimes they manage to live long enough to see the freeing of their nation . . . "

"Professor, . . . dreamers live in a time beyond mine . . . in palaces beyond the seven mountains of folktale . . . and I . . . even if I hang on long enough to see the time they're dreaming of, I'll still see them as Keepers of the Keys, Guardians, Gardeners . . . and there'll be nothing left but for me to walk along those avenues . . . and . . . and to keep bowing from the waist to those Wardens . . . But let me deviate by one step, let me pull a wry face because a flower doesn't smell right—in no time I'll be battered by their key chains."

"Because you're afraid of law and order . . . of nature's order . . . of health . . . You prefer a world drooling with secretions . . . festering."

"Like the birch tree, like the body, like the thaw that makes valleys fertile with slime! . . . My dear man . . . sometimes I see you from a distance, pushing that carriage with those heads in it . . . And what does it all come to? For you, these are sentimental relics, Chinese lanterns, mummers' Herod-masks . . . *I* don't know what they are, but they're not people on easy terms with their own bodies. Just take a closer look at these brainpans. They used to live on good terms with the body. They defended the body's freedom—that's to say, its right to reach for happiness. These brainpans . . . listen . . . before a third heart attack punches me like a rabbit behind the ear . . . You won't meet a happier man in the world than me." (And he laughs, and his laugh gets vulgar and impudent.) "It was dusk, same as now. I went out into the street so as not to listen to the communiqués from Spain in the café . . . You know Paris, when dusk's like it is now . . . in that little street . . . never mind, it'll come back to me . . . I saw two boys on the other side of the road. They're nudging each other, fooling about. They cross over from side to side—and it's all for my benefit. I go past them and see that one's perhaps fifteen and the other at most thirteen. I go past them, and the older one says:

"'Maybe you're looking for someone? We'll be pleased to help . . . '

"'You're too young to help me,' I say, but I look them in the eye.

"The older one smiles so knowingly at this that I no longer have any doubts. But you know, I'm afraid of a trap.

So I keep on walking, and the younger one says:

"'We have a room nearby, at an old aunt's . . . she's deaf as a post . . . Maybe you'll drop in for a visit, we'll have something to drink . . . we're inviting you.'

"After a while we were sitting in a typical Parisian closet, not too shabby, with geraniums at the window. After a while I sent the younger one for bread, ham, and wine. When we'd eaten, we wiped our mouths. 'And what now,' I think to myself. But at this point the older one gets up and turns the key in the door:

"'Let's get undressed, as the gentleman must surely be in a hurry,' he says to the younger one.

"And before I know it, I've got stripped scamps on either side . . . you know, not a bit shy as you might imagine. They take me by the hand and put it first here, then there on their own territory . . . Well, at this point I get undressed as well.

"'Which do you want first, me or my little brother?' asks the older one.

"'What's that? He gives handouts, too, already?' I ask.

"'Certainly,' the elder brother answers for him. 'Right, Jeannot?'

"And the one on the far side smiles but seems a bit unsure of himself. 'I'm learning from him . . . '

"And so as to prove this child's already on the right road . . . the elder buggers him under my eyes and winks from above the youngster to imply I shan't regret it. But I took the older one . . . Man . . . it was a wedding straight out of paradise . . . man . . . we rapscallioned ourselves to a standstill that time . . . they played the pigsty on me, because I told them to do a series of little tricks, till we were dripping with sweat and laughing till we cried . . . because you know, they . . . I was their make-believe father . . . "

I wanted to say something. He noticed the movement of my lips.

"Wait . . . in a minute you'll say what's building up steam inside you . . . I can see that . . . I've nearly finished . . . After all this I leave them and go into the street. I turn into the boulevard. And there they're selling a special edition with a horrendous yell. To the effect that some new Spanish town had been captured or bombed . . . I can't remember anymore. And in the same place jazz gushes out from the doorway of a cellar where there's dancing. The crowd breathes in time to this razzmatazz, and night's spreading over the crowd . . . And beyond the night—God's universe turns in the well-regulated Swiss manner . . . man—and for two hours I'd been so *free* of this world of crime going under the name of law and order, free from this herd instinct of theirs going under the name of progress, everything measured on the same bloody scale . . . I . . . I was fairly rolling along . . . "

"On the down-gradient to the gutter, you mean!"

" . . . I was rolling along under my own steam . . . "

I look at him, and he's waiting for me to attack. He's smiling already. He sees my hands already at work on getting range and elevation with an antiaircraft gun pointed toward Parisian skies through which their gray striped mattress dashes, and on it the threesome of prisoners escaping from my world of people dedicated to war and peace, wrongs and requitals, when the judges will be ourselves. We're grouped here looking at that ark of egoists from which—see, this very minute, they're pouring red wine onto our muzzles . . .

But we're lying down flanking the tracks where there's a terrified train, and outside it SS men like paper because the requital is being written across the sky of Europe in allied script. Because the Lord God Himself wouldn't have created such beautiful skies roaring with compassionate liberators. I look at him because all of a sudden the land of Europe's buckled, so many soldiers are stepping onto it coming up from the sea. And already I've got my mouth full of a white English roll . . . And these soldiers, they're weeping over my hundred pounds, while I'm trembling with the shame of being such an animal. I look at Rudolf with the eyes of that former head, the preprofessorial one. He sees snow falling on it, on its KZ recruit's nakedness. And he just nods his head, as if he were letting a dead brother have his way at the end of a traditional quarrel about a childish toy from sixty years ago.

"And that Hun of yours? What d'you call him—Rudolf . . . doesn't he mean to come here?"

"Mam, he's not alive any longer."

"You see, I had this foreboding . . . I even said a Hail Mary for him—yesterday, I think it was. You wrote to me that you'd taken him apart. I'd have done the same. Well, now you'll have peace from all that writing . . . It's not right to do that, not with children . . . You know what . . . that old billy goat across the way . . . "

"Poptiu?"

"Poptiu, what a swine . . . used to ask kids to his cellar, too . . . He used to give them apples . . . you know, those smashing winter croppers he'd keep in straw. But in return they had to unbutton that huge fly of his, pull his butcher's shop right out, and play with the lot . . . Now, now, don't make out you're disgusted . . . You and that German never used to play . . . discuss tricks like that. But just a minute—didn't you mean to go there?"

And I'm standing glassed in by an orangery and listening to the wind. One minute it strikes with old-style Uhlan cavalry hooves, the next it spurts like modern coal dust until the nasturtiums which are up to my waist recoil, fleshy mouths agape.

It's time, I think to myself, to assemble these smiles running wild over me into one face. And I turn myself along with that face toward the pale waxes of night hives from which my principalities claim their descent. And with my hand I point to this tale full of handrails. Please, after you.

A visit to a friend is an excursion to the shrubbery where, in a well-known snowball tree, a nest is growing more and more spherical from year to year. Different from a bird's because it's enclosed on all sides so that the ball of light inside is more conjectural than verifiable, a mistletoe ball that we nourish each year with new life from a hand warm as milk when its fresh whiteness whispers out into a milk pail.

The pleasure of capturing your own human self in sentences, the self pulsating with tenderness toward a friend. The pleasure of postponing the thrill that runs through two upstanding bodies, when both he and I lay a hand on the nest I described a moment ago, I, inhabitant of Absurdia condemned to play a citizen's role in the republic of Faith, Hope, and Charity.

I pointed out just now the story's land ahead, but my hand got caught up in the sails, entangled in lyrical spider's web, and all because of that nest which has come into being between me and Rudolf like some planet. And now tell the story to your mother, utter such a peroration that your high-flown words whine like flies in a bottle, till out of this whining and clanking a train's thundered out right up to . . .

"You know, Mam, that little town and then by bus to the district where there are those apartment blocks. There's Rudolf's bench against the wall. The entrance hall just as usual in apartment blocks, with little boxes for letters and names on the doors.

"Here it is. I knock. But not a sound after that. Nothing. And suddenly the door edges back, back, and a gray-haired woman—from her face, his sister for sure—is looking me over. I don't remember now what I said. But I can see she's recognized me, that's to say, she knows very well who I am. I can see it in the movement of her hand. You know, Mam, . . . such an all-embracing gesture to invite me in . . . as though she were always opening new doors . . . "

"Well, and then what? Did you kiss her hand?"

" . . . but she doesn't drop her arm and keeps standing like that, neither hospitable nor appealing. So I walk in the direction her hand's pointing, and by this time I'm preparing my face for a surprise, for my Rudolf's popping out from behind a door! I'm getting my eyes ready for the reception of his urchin's look, his look sprinkled with cornflower vodka. I've gone as far as a wall and have to turn around. And I see that she's lowering her hand slowly and I hear: 'What are you looking for? Can't you see that I'm alone? My husband died a month ago.'

"I was dumbfounded. My hands dropped limply on my belly and my mouth fell open . . . and now all of a sudden the apartment's full of fir trees, of jays with black and blue braiding, of mistletoe in fruit with December teardrops. We stand, widow and friend, without anything to guide us in the presence of these not-leaves-not-bees battering themselves against corners like birds, and I'm odd man out, I'm odd man out . . .

"And all at once I fling myself at the window and push it wide open. And all at once my hand's gone up of its own volition and pointed at the sky. And—you know, Mam—those jay's feathers, geraniums, and bats, those mistletoes along with my stupefied petrified silence . . . they've clustered together into a kind of . . . a kind of fleshy pumpkin and tally ho! flown out through the window like sound, like sand, or like tattered odds and ends . . .

"And through this very same window a sweaty July's crept in. So that the silence is sticky under your armpits. And so I say to the widow:

"'And now what?'

"'I shall go to my son, near the Swiss border, because I have nobody here . . . '

"She's said this, and she's eyeing me with satisfaction. Because I'm a simpleton. Because Rudolf's led me up the creek. And because she can look pityingly at Professor Prickski who's not up to snuff."

"Pour one for me and one for yourself," says our Mam. "Laddie . . . what does that make him . . . this Rudolf of yours . . . one arse for sale in two markets?"

I pinch the edge of the tiny liqueur glass with my lips and screw up my eyes, making out that this absinth is too bitter with wormwood, but I feel silly looking into the woman's eyes of my mother who shakes her gray head sadly, a little concerned about this Rudolf who's been promoted overzealously by her son. And so I return hastily to the widow.

"'And now what?' I ask her, because the hag's given me a poor answer, 'what now?'

And the widow brings her bike from the hall. Now we're
    past the last apartment
here where toadstools are growing in each small allotment
along with constipated gnomes set in cement
where a pensioner is trying to cough up his phlegm
under those lilac bushes there's some kind of movement
a foreign worker no doubt scrubbing some
local girl in white-collar employment
he's head downward
she's feet upward
and by now we're beside the wall of the graveyard
Rudolf's widow pedaling, a woman
with knees tucked into a black garment
while inside its shoe my big toe's all but scarred.

"She's pedaling and doesn't so much as look at me because she knows I'm following her with a dignified gait, professorial, neatly pressed, buttoned right up to the last button of my fly.

"It seems as if she's speeded up, because I'm aware of her widow's sweat."

Our Mam gesticulates with her hand as a sign that something's amused her.

"Laddie, you're forever and always like that—on foot while those womenfolk of yours are on cycles . . . "

And she sees that I see my first love pedaling till her Nivea-anointed calves gleam against a background of shimmering holiday air. She sees that I see her stopping at the garden gate, so that I can tilt her saddle with its leather beak upward, so that I can make it firm with a spanner in a snub-nosed fucking position. And while, kneeling, I'm screwing up, screwing home, she's yawning with her entire body. When I'm panting and standing up, red from proximity to her calves, thanked and given my quittance . . . she's already straddling the saddle, absorbing it, and vanishing so that only the air, whipped crosswise by her pigtail, comes back in a zigzag . . . and . . .

"Quick, because the bike of my-not-my widow's got bogged down in German sand. I push her by her saddle, oooff! now we're on firm ground. And downhill all the way, let her rush along alone, stubborn in her hag-ridden gray hairs till she all but runs over a grave into two little flowerbeds from which fancy pansies look at us bleary-eyed, Mongolian fashion.

"She looks me in the eyes. And talks to me with these auger-peepers and doesn't mince her speaking looks:

"'Well—you've got your Rudolf, have a nice chat with each other, you worm-eaten pricks.'

"And she stares me insolently in the face. But I wet my index finger with a little spit and comb my right eyebrow, so that it's green and magpielike all of a sudden. And the same with the other eyebrow. And I execute a circle in the air with my hand as if I'm flourishing a cane, as if I'm one of those rare dandies, as if there's a carnation in my buttonhole . . . And I stare at her over my shoulder, smiling indulgently at this female bumpkin who's pretending she can't see my curly fair hair or my nostrils flaring that scent already mentioned. I bestow a chilly smirk on this bumpkin seamstress who doesn't notice about three hundred maple leaves whirling above me . . . And I sense that the hag's getting smaller, fatter, that pretty soon she'll start to grunt close by my shoe and wallow in the sand of the new grave . . . Baah!

"Meanwhile, her eyes have cleared unexpectedly. A kind

of dignity's made her mouth beautiful, and I hear:

"'My husband wanted a son very much. After our marriage we settled down in a small timbered manor house on the edge of a forest teeming with stags . . . The landowner had gone off somewhere, so this manor and forest were left in our care. There were berries galore, you know, we were always eating wild strawberries that a servant girl drenched in endless cream . . . My husband who's passed on insisted I should eat wild strawberries because there's iron in them. On Sunday we'd whisk up ice creams, you know, raspberry ones . . . Sometimes Olek would take us to Warsaw in the carriage to buy this and that.'

"And she's looking at me insolently again: would you believe it? She thinks she's some kind of lady of the manor because she's got a little cunt, because Rudolf fancied having a son . . . And what's this fellow to me, she seems to ask. What am I doing here?"

"But, laddie, couldn't you . . . talk back at her the way we do?! What right had she to cut you down to size, making a fool of you . . . "

"Hmm . . . hmmm . . . you know, Mam . . . by now I'm beginning to be on my guard against graveyards . . . because I've heard of so many strange happenings and shocking deeds done on graves by now that I've not only stopped trusting other people but myself, too, when I start telling tales in company about graveyard incidents. Mam, you've heard about Smorodina . . . "

"A wretch."

"You see what I mean, Mam . . . so I look meekly at my sandy shoes as though I'm convinced by this manor of hers, its hearth strewn with wild strawberries, but slowly, very slowly I raise my head and unpurse my lips:

"'Oh, these manor houses . . . Madam . . . you go inside and in a flash it's full of mirrors . . . you can scarcely turn around without meeting staircases and a handrail made of red-brown resinous pine wood . . . When there's a snow-storm turning gray over the fields, all you need to do is wind up the gramophone and look at the fireplace with its birch logs changing color . . . Riiight? And invite a houseful of guests, making sure they're crooks, pricks, Cossacks in boots up to their balls! And douse them in a halo of schnapps. Why I assure you, Madam, real-life boars will emerge from the dark forest and come along with their hairy wives up to the windows, breathe on them with their boarish breath so as to admire this resplendent ball. Riiight? Madam—I was there, drank vodka and danced a polka, then out once more, arse first and head after . . . '

"And she—you know, Mam—starts to gnaw her lip because she's getting the feeling she won't make a mug of me so easily with this cosy little husband . . . and that I know a thing or two about this manor . . .

"But in spite of this she brazens it out:

"'What can you know about manors then? Only what you read in books!'

"But I look at her, Mam, and start to nod my head ironi-cally, in that way we know in our parts when instead of say-ing like a home-grown pedagogue talking to kids: 'You know about arses, you've seen the shit,' we simply nod and hold fire. And I nod at this widow with her wild strawber-ries in mourning colors, and hold my fire . . . And next minute she makes out, as it were, she must put something to rights on the grave of her late landed proprietor, crouches down and pushes sand about as if I wasn't really there beside her, as if she and her sorrow were in league and I'm an intruder . . . So I bend down and—in a gentle voice like you taught me, Mam, I croon:

"'Careful! Yees, you can smooth down here, plant this and that . . . here as well, but *not here!*' And I point at the middle of the grave with a hand solemn as Chopin's funeral march transfixed by frost.

"'*Nein, so das!* Well, really . . . ' She's become so indignant she's begun to hiss! And she looks at me. And rises from her squatting position so as to be more impressive.

"'Not here,' I repeat, 'because it's beyond the pale to hide the name that's underground, that's like spring in green letters on Rudolf's body!'

"And I kneel on both knees at the foot of the grave and with my finger, which knows all tongues by heart, I write in the sand:

YAZIT

"And the widow, like a dishcloth after a soaking in bleach, lifts her hand and moans, '*Weg da!*' But she's shaking. As though she's driving me out of this private graveyard. She's trying to play at being a female archangel. But I don't get up from my kneeling position and don't do anything all this time, except with my finger, my vast finger stick, I keep digging this proclamation deeper and deeper . . . "

Our Mam screws up her eyes and shrugs her shoulders, pursing her lips:

"You know . . . give over, do . . . really, humiliating yourself like that in front of a foreign woman . . . floundering about in sand on all fours . . . for goodness sake . . . Wasn't it up to her to throw herself on that grave?! You're a professor! To lower yourself like that . . . You getting involved with that thingamajig of hers—nothing wrong with that. I've seen his photo, he had the right sort of look in his eyes and used to stand up for Poles . . . But what's that hussy of his got to offer?! Who do you take after, accosting it doesn't matter who, getting into conversation, asking all about their family even when they tell you they haven't got a family . . . I know. She got through to you with those wild strawberries. Just show you three berries—you forget about your doctorate on the spot, and you'd feed cows with whoever, and you'd sing like a ploughboy draped in a horse blanket like those horse herders, you know, on the banks of the San . . . Before the war you put yourself in Kobylecki's hands to set you on just the right road . . . hang on, what was it he used to say? . . . because you used to repeat it to me . . . oh yes . . . 'I go into the graveyard, old chap, into ink-black night . . . not a living soul. Only corpses, shoulder to shoulder. I wait for them to start haunting me, but it's quiet here . . . Bah, I said, fine ghosts *you* are! I turned on my heel, old chap; they won't see me there anymore.' It made me smile then, because you'd smeared yourselves with that ink of yours like two kids in a nursery . . . Do give over . . . Pour us another one each, laddie . . . Listen, you live there in the capital, you've got gold opera glasses . . . what??? you haven't? Buy some! As soon as you get back buy opera glasses and hold them like this in your right hand. And go slowly down stairs carpeted in something red . . . glancing now left, now right. Over there you've still got opera, a king and a queen—take advantage of it all, be on the alert, let them think to themselves: 'That must be a Pole because he's holding his head up so high.' Well, never mind, you can laugh, you rascal, if it weren't for my Hail Marys you wouldn't have come alive out of those trenches, those incinerated ashes, those sanatorium consumptions . . . No need to kiss an old woman . . . Well, that's enough. Shut the door, you see, that old witch's dog from over the fence is barking already . . . But just you write . . . And get married, you rascal."

Words have their own home. There are no swallows without a roof, without a shore from which they launch themselves in flight. A cloud of July bees on a visit to swooning garden walks has its home, a home for the night, with its rules and natural rhythms.

And the little song I can hear inside my head here, by a canal in Bruges, owes its origin to Domaradz, to a tavern bursting at the seams with the bawling of ploughboys, to a rowdy wedding. From such places—oh show me the way to go home—come my colloquial words and this gool, this ghyll, this hecky. I take care of them, feed them, and help them to take wing, applauding the noisy dance all on my own, exiled bird fancier of words that keep faith with me. I run under them with a pathetic length of yarn in my hand while they circle like a paper kite, carry me across the years like a garrulous parachute; we are fathers and mothers to each other, orphans with heads held high.

At this time of year nothing's in flower any longer. The acacias stand idle save for a pigeon that's found a place for a nap, swollen with wheat. Under the trees are stones, some laid flat, others upright, and on these stones are a number of people engraved with chisel and shade. Here and there, pre-war marble lies like a black chest all set for a voyage across the ocean, but mostly just beds of flowers walled round, with a visiting card like a little pillow at the head, or fastened to the ground by a rusty cross until the last amen.

The air is clammy and motionless. Rain beyond the mountain. One look and it'll leap across and start pouring.

From somewhere or other you can hear a shovel screeching as it mixes concrete slurry with gravel for a new grave plot. And now a bus steps on the gas because it's got to go uphill to town.

But on his way from town, shielding his long nose from exhaust fumes with a scented handkerchief, a sixty-year-old man is going down toward the old cemetery. He's gone in under the trees briskly, but almost at once slackens his pace, looks round, then sets off again, "yes, it's in that row," till he reaches a hedge of wild roses and a heap of weeds and branches thrown down there so as to make compost. No, it's not here. "Patience," he thinks to himself, and works out a method of systematic search, accepts his own proposal, and turns back with relief to the same paths as a moment before, repeating the same names . . . starts shaking his head helplessly . . . and there it is!

Beyond monuments, beyond storied stone vaults—a small, fresh flowerbed on the level. And next to it another with its wall of cement already round it. He's taken off his hat. Wipes brow and nape with his handkerchief. And looks at this local clay, packed down into a prism by the sexton's spade. And looks at the fern that's already had time to take. He tries to botch together some solemn aphorism, but the bricklayer's shovel jars in his gray-haired head. A new bus has hooted his thoughts in half. He looks at the clay and only now recalls that he's brought candles from abroad. Meeting of hand with earth. Pressing in of violet candles. Absurd little flames at high noon. His eyes are full of this winking violetry; he scatters it over the grave and then slowly stands up, and sees that clay is clay and he's himself.

But he doesn't see that nine graves to the east, behind a vault made of terrazzo for thirty thousand złotys, freshly polished, two heads lurk in ambush pressed down close to the roof, behind the walling up to their teeth so that only their eyes keep a lookout.

They've chosen a good spot. Downwind so the hare won't scent their stool-pigeon sweat. They can even whisper breathily to each other because, in any case, the shovel blends and blends all sounds into chocolate cake mixed with ash . . .

"He's very thoughtful."

"He's praying."

"Pray, *him!!!* But maybe? Who knows what's going on inside . . . "

"Look, look!"

"He's combing his hair. Combing it in front of the grave!! He's straightening his tie!"

"What's 'this? He's put his hands behind his back and . . . "

" . . . and he's strolling about as though he were in a posh room!"

"He's smiling . . . "

"He's shaking his head . . . "

"As if to say 'that's not done,' . . . "

"Look. He's spinning her some yarn."

"He's laughing so much, you can see his gold teeth!"

"He's bending his head down . . . "

"Yes he is . . . as if he were waiting for an answer . . . "

"Loony . . . oh look! He's climbing up on the steps of that tomb . . . "

"What's he got in his hand? Good grief! Not a knife, surely?!"

"Nooo! It's catching the light . . . a watch . . . he must have a train to catch . . . no."

"He's holding it in front of him and putting on proper gent's airs for the grave's benefit!"

"Good grief . . . hope his brains haven't scrambled . . . "

"My God . . . "

"Oh look . . . he's putting it up to his eyes . . . why, it's—opera glasses!"

"Quiet, don't shout!"

"*I'm* shouting?! It's you that's yelling fit to bust . . . "

"Hide, because any minute he might . . . "—and they both hide behind their terrazzo pigsty.

After a moment one leans out, then the other, and they look at the newcomer loosening his tie, stooping down, plucking a fern frond from the grave and putting it in his buttonhole. Now he's evidently felt the first drop on his bald patch, because he's stretching his hand skyward but next minute lowers it . . .

And there's no longer any need to point out or make sure of anything, because the rain's leapt over the woods and is here now, rushing across meadows, kitchen gardens, the noise of it growing from strength to strength until it's a regular deluge. So that even the clay, the mud this man was fooling with a short while ago, is shining, even the stones acquire a sheen, the ones lying prone and the ones standing upright. Till even the bricklayer's fled under a juniper with his shovel and even the pigeon on the acacia has tucked his head into his gray feathers.

Then the newcomer puts his hat on his head, starts

swinging his arms in readiness for a long march, but before he takes a step, he squats down again by the grave. He's up to something there, but nobody's spying on him any longer, keeping an eye on him, hunting him down, because the rain's smoked out the Peeping Toms.

He rises from his knees. He stretches his muddy right hand out in front of him, not quite begging a favor, not quite pointing at the mountains, and he moves off along the path, so battered by rain that at the cemetery exit his palm's white again. So that no one will read his last gesture off it.

And he's not making for the town but for the park on the hill. And not by way of the main entrance—like that time he went walking through the night after a wretched smoked fish—but he clambers uphill across a pathless tract. He's twisted his hat round so it squints zanily at his shoulders. He's walking with knees bent. And so like a buffoon, trailing and trawling his feet uphill, following the drift of the driving rain that's been pelting down and is now giving the town a silver whipping.

And from that fern cutting grafted on his buttonhole—a May garland already, a hunchback garland round his body. So that there's no professor but a toad spurting its own laughter.

And by this time the flood's passing him by, rushing through the sky. And once again the air's wide open. So much so that the sun's a mass of buttery maize in the sky-blue bowl of a reaper from the farmhands' quarters. And below, in the valley's hollow—the town has burst into speech. Children have scattered from the schoolhouse, and each one has a cake in his hand. And off they go, trundling resolutely round the schoolyard. A train's run out from behind a hill so that you can hear its lungs. And the peasant women in the marketplace—bring eggs out from under their skirts, one, two, three in succession, nice and white and dry. And heap them up in pyramids. And their menfolk do the same with red-hot potatoes that they pull from inside their jackets. But the teacher's already clapping her hands, and the children in the schoolyard are already forming up in a pattern, stretching out their little arms in the shape of a cross, standing on one leg and reciting in such a way that this golden treasury of words can be poured in pots for winter. Soldiers pelted with flowers come from among the pyramids, white and red Polish pyramids. Their goosestep draws them on into the distance till at last, as if turned to a pillar of salt, each bereft left leg stays stuck up in the air. And despite the effort that's written on their faces, despite more and more voluble curses, in no way can they haul that leg down again.

And on the hill, salvaged just now from the sky's deluge, without straightening his bowed legs, the hunchbacked stranger clasps the newborn light and, pumpkin by pumpkin, sets it on the ground. And all of them, too, in their succulent spheres, heap themselves up into a pyramid.

See—now he's lifted his arms and at this sign
has toppled everything that he's assembled.
And you can hear the town under the battery
of pumpkins muttering, merrily rioting
and shattering
in a rush, a gush of wild red honey, ruddy good honey,
rudolf.

The End

■ □ ■ □ ■

WRITINGS FROM AN UNBOUND EUROPE